Jennifer

Also by David Helwig

FICTION

The Streets of Summer
The Day Before Tomorrow
The King's Evil

THE KINGSTON NOVELS

The Glass Knight
A Sound Like Laughter
It is Always Summer

DOCUMENTARY

A Book About Billie

POETRY

Figures in a Landscape
The Sign of the Gunman
The Best Name of Silence
Atlantic Crossings
A Book of the Hours

Jennifer

~ *A Novel* ~

DAVID HELWIG

BEAUFORT BOOKS, INC.
New York

Library of Congress Cataloging in Publication Data

Helwig, David, 1938-
Jennifer.

I. Title.
PR9199.3.H445J4   1983   813'.54   83-3772
ISBN 0-8253-0148-3

Published in the United States by Beaufort Books, Inc.,
New York.
Printed in the U.S.A.   First Edition
10 9 8 7 6 5 4 3 2 1

For Nancy, with love

We must not pursue complexity nor great variety in the basic movements, but must observe what are the rhythms of a life that is orderly and brave . . .

—Plato, *The Republic.*

I

Alone in the kitchen while the lives of her children went on around her in the other rooms of the house, Jennifer stood for a moment and looked out the window where the last light of the early autumn day was gathered in the pale streaks of the cloudy sky. It seemed to her that she was growing happily into the habit of solitude, at least the special kind of solitude of a woman alone with her children. She felt her own separateness more strongly in the face of what she had just heard on the phone, Barbara announcing awkwardly, almost shyly, that she was in the general hospital, the mental ward, having that morning cut her wrists. Visiting hours ended at eight. To make it, Jennifer would have to leave the dishes on the counter and do them later.

Gavin came around the kitchen door.

"Did you hear about the butcher who backed into the meat-slicer and got a little behind in his work?"

"Go and do your homework."

"I'm finished."

"Well, find something else to keep you out of trouble. I have to go over to the hospital for a little while."

"Who's in the hospital?"

"Mrs. Walker."

"What's the matter with her?"

Barbara's son, Jeg (the name was a family contraction of his real names, James Gregory) was a friend of Gavin's from school; Jennifer and Barbara had met through the boys. Jennifer found herself tongue-tied by Gavin's question, not knowing what Jeg would know or be told.

"I don't know," she said as the smallest of lies and least of traps. She could adapt her story later.

"Is she very sick?"

"She phoned me."

"Probably went in to have her tubes tied."

5

He looked so assured as he said it, playing adult as he often tried to do since Robert had left. It hurt her that he should have to do this, but she was touched by his bravery. The assumed poise, the incessant jokes; there was something fierce and lovely behind them. She pinched his ear.

"Beat it."

She looked around the kitchen to see if there was anything the cat was likely to knock down. Put the butter up in the cupboard. All too often when she was about to butter a slice of bread, she noticed ridged marks where Bena's tongue had licked it. Jennifer was not very fond of Bena, a large fluffy grey cat who had appeared at the door one day, to Cindy's delight, and had stayed since.

As Jennifer was closing the cupboards, there was a knock at the front door. Damn. Not now. It was 7.30, and Barbara was expecting her. There was no knowing how badly off she was. When she opened the front door, hoping it was something that could be dismissed or put off, she saw, with a sinking heart, that it was Eugene Slyfield, one of the mental patients who sometimes came to chat with her at work. He stood on the dark porch, smiling, boyish, in a mood of completely unconvincing cheerfulness.

She couldn't face Eugene. Not now.

"Can I come in?"

She held the door for him, wanting to say No, but unable to do it. It was too unkind to send him away when he'd come all this way to see her. But why had he come? It was the first time she'd seen him outside the framework of the psychiatric hospital, and she was put off balance by the newness of the circumstance. He walked past her and into the living-room. She followed.

"Can I sit down?"

"Eugene ..."

"You don't want me here." Sudden, challenging.

"It's not that."

"You're afraid I'll do my nut act, frighten the children,

6

aren't you Jennifer?"

"No."

"Why not? Don't you think it would frighten the children? You've never seen me when I get really bad. I feel as if I might get really bad tonight."

He was threatening her. The light from a lamp caught the scar on his forehead. She didn't know what the scar was from. It looked ominous.

"I guess I should just go away."

"Eugene, I'm not really myself tonight. A friend of mine tried to commit suicide this morning. I have to go and see her."

"Don't let me keep you from seeing your friend. I realize that our relationship is simply professional. I'm used to that. All my relationships are very professional. I'm a professional patient. A career schizophrenic, just like in Ronnie Laing. But Ronnie's a romantic. He thinks he's Shelley. Being crazy is much more boring than that. 'It's hackneyed words, its homicidal eye.' That's from Robert Lowell. He did time in a nut-house too."

"I know."

"Yes. I forget that you're literate. I'm sorry. I'm being difficult. Could I just sit down for a minute?" The bravado had disappeared from his face.

"All right, for a minute, but I have to get there before eight. I promised."

"Dear Jennifer, who never breaks promises. I mean that kindly."

"Good."

"They don't know I'm here."

"Should you phone?"

"I'll go back in a little while. They let me out during the day. No reason I shouldn't be out after dark, is there? Will I turn into a werewolf?"

"I guess not."

"I guess not. Where are your children?"

7

"Upstairs."

"How old are they?"

"Cindy's thirteen. Gavin's eleven."

"Cindy's thirteen. Has she started to menstruate yet?"

He was looking her in the eye as if the question was a challenge. He had no right to interrogate her like this, but somehow she had given him the opportunity by being friendly, by opening the door to him. He mustn't see she was frightened.

"Yes, she has."

"Good. I read somewhere that the earlier people reach sexual maturity, the more highly sexed they are. I think that highly sexed people have a happier life. I think they're more fulfilled, don't you?"

He was staring toward her, the straight blond hair going back at an angle that exaggerated the scar. His lips were short and thick, and he had a habit of pursing them.

Jennifer just shrugged in response to his question. She wanted him out of the house, regretted that she had ever met or spoken to him at the hospital.

"Are you highly sexed?" he said.

"Pretty normal, I think."

"What's normal?"

Again she shrugged. Her fear was beginning to paralyze her. Eugene was thin, but he had broad shoulders, and his hands looked strong. As if in response to her glance, his fingers began to move. One hand scratched the back of the other.

"I'm a voluntary patient. I can leave any time I feel like it. I just go in when I'm having trouble and come back out again when I feel stronger. There's really nothing wrong with me except that I get depressed. Why did your friend try to commit suicide?"

"I don't know."

"You'd better go and see her. Unhappy people take promises very seriously. For instance, you promised me that

8

I could come here, and I've been relying on it. Do you realize that?"

"Yes."

"We project our disturbance on the environment, so we're always looking for someplace to escape."

"But you know you can't."

"I don't. Maybe it really is in the environment. If I lived here with you, I might be perfectly all right."

Jennifer was unable to respond. The room seemed crowded, airless. How could she get him out? He was stronger than she was and more determined.

"Do you have many friends in town?" she said.

"Are you frightened of me?"

"No." She didn't think it carried much conviction.

"You shouldn't be. I like you. You're very intelligent. I don't know how you can put up with those freaks you work with."

"Why do you call them that?"

"That's what they are. They look strange and they make odd noises. I think that would come under the definition of freak, if you cared to look it up."

"They're just children with difficult problems."

"Do you have anything to drink?"

"No." She hoped he didn't decide to look for himself.

"I'm not supposed to drink, but I do sometimes. I always think it might be going to do something for me, but usually it just makes me morose. I'm lousy when I'm morose. Even more boring than usual. Am I boring you?"

"I told you I'm preoccupied. Because of my friend."

"Do you attract self-destructive people to you?"

"I've never thought so."

"I think you do. The first time I noticed you at the nut-farm, I thought I wanted to meet you. There was something about you, I don't know what. You're a very exceptional woman, Jennifer."

"Not really."

9

"Did you say you were divorced?"

"Yes."

"Is your former husband a self-destructive person?"

"Perhaps."

"You see what I mean. We're drawn to you. There's something special, I mean I wouldn't ever want to hurt you. Because you're special."

Jennifer tried to steal a look at her wrist-watch. He saw her.

"You want me to go, don't you?"

"Another time I'd be able to concentrate better."

"Is she a very close friend, I mean really close? Do you tell her all your secrets?"

"No."

"What do you talk to her about?"

"I don't know. Children, what we're doing, nothing special."

"Do you talk about your sex lives?"

"No."

"I'd talk about my sex life if there was anything to talk about. Masturbation isn't a very popular topic. There's not much to be said about it, is there? Jig, jig, jig. That's it. Does your son masturbate yet?"

"I don't know."

"My mother was scared to death of it. Scared to death. I used to pretend I was doing it under the table when she had guests. Jig, jig, jig. She got red in the face and looked the other way. I always enjoyed tormenting her. She wasn't a strong person like you."

Jennifer glanced at her watch. She must get him to leave, but she couldn't somehow bring the words to her lips. She was afraid of him and afraid of hurting him.

"Does your daughter go out with boys?"

"No. Not yet."

"I saw her as I was coming to the house. Through one of the windows upstairs. She was standing looking out. I liked her hair. It was very poetic to see her standing like that in the light. At the window. And I was out in the dark coming to visit you. It seemed like a poem, like something out of a poem, this pure young girl at the window, and I was coming here."

"I really have to go," Jennifer said and stood up.

"I'll just wait here until you get back."

The answer she had dreaded receiving. Somehow she had to get him out of the house.

"You don't trust me to stay here, do you?" he said.

"The children don't know you, and I think they'd be nervous left alone with a stranger."

Go. Get out. Please go away.

"Introduce me first. I'm really quite good with children. I don't really feel as if I'll get bad tonight. I can tell. I just said that to see if you got upset. I'll be okay."

"Maybe you could come back later."

"Don't throw me out. Please."

He looked young and vulnerable. For a moment Jennifer was tempted. Someone had to take him in.

"No," she said. "I'm afraid you'll have to go."

He sat in the chair, silent, sullen, not looking at her, his whole body communicating hostility as surely as if it had grown barbs or quills. As she looked toward him, his figure seemed dark, foreign, for a moment covered with fur. Who is the mad one here? she thought. Hang on. Get him out.

"Eugene, you'll have to go now."

"I won't hurt your precious children."

"I'm sure you wouldn't, but I can't leave you here."

"You can't put me out on the street."

"I'll call a cab to take you back."

"I won't go back. I'm not ever going back. I'm going to go home. My mother said I could always come home if I wanted. She didn't mean it, but she said it, so tomorrow I'm going home. Back to Ottawa."

His head was turned to the corner of the room, but his

11

eyes were looking back toward Jennifer.

"Please go now, Eugene."

"You invited me here."

"No I didn't. I said maybe you could come sometime."

"I took that as an invitation."

"All right, yes, I suppose it was. And you can come back another time, later on this evening if you like."

"I had a dream last night with you in it. It was one of those dreams where you can't touch anything. And everyone I saw was melting and turning into a pool that I was swimming through, but they kept sticking to me, pieces like arms and legs kept sticking to me. You were over at one side of the pool, and I kept thinking that if I could get close enough you'd pull me out, but then you turned your back to me because you were doing something you didn't want me to see. . . ."

"Eugene . . ." She tried to make her voice sound firm, but she was afraid it was only shrill. "You have to go now. Do you want me to call a cab?"

He hunched down in the chair.

"Do you think you're strong enough to throw me out?" he said.

She looked down at him. There was a burning sensation at the back of her eyes, and she was afraid she'd begin to cry. She wondered if the children could hear the voices, could hear what was being said. What if Gavin decided to come and help her? He was so small.

"I'll have to call the police, Eugene."

She picked up the phone and began to dial. Eugene jumped from the chair and ran toward her. As he grabbed the phone and pushed her away from it with his shoulder, she found her leg caught in the cord. As she fell, she put out her arm to catch herself, scraped her wrist on the doorjamb, then felt a jolt all the way up her arm as her weight came down on her wrist. Eugene stood with the phone in his hand, looking down at her. Jennifer sat on the floor beneath

12

him, her back to the wall. Neither one moved.

Jennifer wanted to get up, but she was afraid to. She tried to plan what she might do next, whether she could grab his legs and knock him over. Could Cindy and Gavin jump out a window?

Eugene hung the receiver back up and put the phone on the table.

"I don't have to go, but I will. Because you want me to. And I know you're a special kind of person. I wouldn't ever hurt you."

He was moving away from her. Jennifer got quickly to her feet. She went out into the hall and began to put on her coat.

"Which way are you walking?" she said. "I'm going down to the General. Do you want to walk over with me?"

Anything to get him out of the house.

"Maybe I could see your friend too. I understand what she must feel like."

"We'll talk about it on the way over."

He was moving toward the door. She tried not to watch him so that he wouldn't feel the pressure of her desire to be rid of him. If he did, he would rebel. He came and stood close to her as she opened the door. There was a curious, almost chemical smell coming from him. Her wrist was still throbbing where she had fallen on it. She reached out to open the door, fixed the button so that it would lock when pulled tight behind her.

Eugene moved toward the door. He was almost out.

"Mum."

It was Cindy's voice from upstairs. Eugene stopped. His body was framed in the doorway, and as he stood there, his eyes turned back toward the voice, and the light caught the scar and outlined it against the dark street behind him. Something came to life in his eyes. Jennifer was rigid for a moment, trapped by the sharp outline against the light, then suddenly she moved, shoved him out the door and pulled and locked it behind her.

"What did you do that for? I wasn't going to hurt her."

"Walk over to the hospital with me," she said. She wanted him gone, but felt she must be careful. She began to move down the steps from the porch. He stood behind her, unmoving.

"Where can I go? I don't have any place to go."

"Why don't you go back to the hospital?"

"You'd like to see me locked up for good, wouldn't you?"

She was several paces away from him now.

"Are you going to walk with me?"

"No. You're just trying to get me away from here. Well, I won't go. I'll stay right here. It's not that easy to get rid of me, Jennifer."

Jennifer kept walking, waiting for a sound, his feet running after her to attack her or the shock of breaking glass as he smashed the window of the house. All she heard was the sound of his voice.

"I'll be waiting here when you come back," he screamed into the night. "I'm the price you pay for being happy."

Quickly to the corner, and once round the corner Jennifer began to run. It was only a few blocks to the hospital, and once inside, she could get to a phone and call Cindy. She was not used to running, and her breath caught in her chest. To reach the hospital, she had to pass several university buildings. By the door of the Students' Union, she saw a girl with long hair and a boy in an engineering jacket holding hands. She wanted to go to them, to send them back to her house. She couldn't ask strangers. It would be all right till she reached the hospital. Would it? The boy looked toward her as she ran by, and she felt angry, resentful at his innocence. She should not have left Eugene on the porch of the house. If he knocked, Cindy might answer. It was too far to the hospital. She crossed Union Street against a red light, and a car nearly hit her.

There must be a telephone close. She didn't know her way around the university buildings, but she recognized one where she had attended concerts. She ran to the door, praying it would be open. It was. She rushed to the pay phone, breathless, fumbling with her coins. Her gestures seemed slow, drunken, the phone took forever to ring. She heard Cindy's voice. She was alive.

"Cindy, has anyone knocked at the door or tried to get in."

"Where are you? What's happening?" There was a whine of childish fear in her voice.

"That boy who came to the door is from the hospital. I had a bit of trouble getting him out of the house, but he's out now, and the door's locked."

"Where are you?"

"I'm at a phone just down the street. Don't worry. Everything will be okay. Can you peek out the window and see if anybody's on the porch or standing on the street in front of the house?"

"Just a minute."

If he was still around, Jennifer decided, she would phone the police and go back to meet them at the house. She could see Barbara tomorrow.

"Mum, I looked, and there's nobody on the porch."

"Did you see anybody out on the lawn or the street?"

"No."

Jennifer stood silent, undecided. The children were more important than anything else, more important than Barbara, but Eugene was gone. The door was locked.

"Will you be okay if I go down to the hospital for a few minutes?"

"Do you have to?"

"I promised. I won't be long. I'll phone as soon as I get there to make sure you're still all right. If anybody comes to the door, don't open it unless you see who it is. If that boy comes back, phone the police. All right?"

"I guess so."

Jennifer hung up. Maybe she should go straight back home. But Barbara had sounded so desperate on the phone, so determined that Jennifer must come and see her. Why did everything happen at once? Jennifer gathered herself together and set out for the hospital. It was no more than a five minutes' walk, and when she arrived, she found a phone and called home again.

"Is everything all right, Cindy?"

"Yeah." She sounded quite cheerful. "I phoned Daddy, and he's going to come over."

"I'll see you in a few minutes," Jennifer said and hung up. An encounter with Robert was the last thing she needed tonight, but she couldn't blame Cindy for phoning him. He was her father. Odd that Jennifer hadn't thought of it, but it had become an essential discipline to keep him out of her mind. She had resolved to ask him for nothing and had taught herself to forget him. He was no longer a part of her or her life. She had only herself now. And the children, a few friends, but they didn't invade or compromise her.

Jennifer checked her watch. Only a few minutes of the visiting hours left. She walked down the long hospital hallway to the elevator. In the rooms on each side of the hall, she caught glimpses of the patients, some surrounded by flowers and visitors, some alone in the bare rooms. The face of an old woman, pale against the white pillow, the eyes staring straight ahead. A card on the table beside the bed. One saw too much in walking through a hospital; the human pain and fear was too naked, too bare, and yet it was curiously exciting. One breathed deeper as if part of a great tragic play. Death walked here, and birth, and the awkwardness of unspeakable love, and all were tied to the complex impersonal apparatus of medicine. When the doctors came here, they put on their white coats and looked wise. Jennifer didn't grudge them their magic. How else live with all this?

As she reached the elevator, a man came out, a man she knew but couldn't name. A dark warm face with curly hair. He looked at her with recognition, half smiled, looked as if he wanted to speak, then decided against it and moved away. Jennifer had seen him at parties and concerts.

She reported to the nursing-station. Barbara wasn't in bed, but in the chair by the window, dressed in one of the plain ugly hospital gowns. She wore no makeup. The skin over the bridge of her nose seemed stretched too tight, and her eyes looked flat and hurt, but all these things served only to increase the beauty of her face, with its pale blue eyes and the fine, perfectly placed bones of nose and cheeks, forehead and chin. The hospital gown was short, and as she turned her body toward Jennifer, it was pulled farther up. Her legs were thin, and purple veins showed under the surface of the pale skin.

Jennifer went to her. Barbara reached out her hands. There were bandages around both her wrists. Jennifer took her hands and squeezed them, sat on the edge of the narrow hospital bed and looked down at her.

"Oh Jenny, it's all such a mess."

"I'm sorry."

"I don't know what I'm going to do."

"Is it Al?"

"No.... Maybe in a way it is."

Barbara's husband was consistently and almost openly unfaithful to her. He was a hotel-manager who found it easy to use his office or a room in the hotel and whose hours were unpredictable enough that he hardly had to make excuses. It was obvious enough what was happening, but Barbara never mentioned it.

"Jenny, I made the world's oldest, stupidest mistake. I fell in love. I figured after all these years, it was my right. After all these years of being the perfect wife and mother, I figured it was my right." She began to pick at one of the bandages on her wrist.

"What happened? Did Al find out?"

"No."

"What?"

"I feel like such a fool. Oh God, I'm so ashamed."

Her sobs were coming up from her stomach and shaking her body like hiccups. She looked up, her face raw with crying and distress. Jennifer couldn't bear to observe such humiliation. She would never have let another woman see her like that.

"I didn't even sleep with him. It's so ridiculous. I feel like a kid. I think that was what I couldn't stand, being like that, just foolish and naive. It's all so childish, cutting my wrists to make him feel sorry." She wiped her eyes, reached for a Kleenex from beside the bed and blew her nose.

"I'm sorry to dump all this on you, Jenny. You're the only one I can talk to. I can't tell Al that I invented a great romance with a man who just meant to be friendly. He thinks I'm depressed from being cooped up with the kids. He's going to take me to Montreal for a week."

"It won't hurt to get away."

"I suppose not. I don't know if I want to spend a week alone with Al. Jenny . . ."

"What?"

"He's the only man I've ever made love to. I guess I'm not one of your more liberated women." She sniffed and smiled. "I'm glad I got to know you, Jenny. I was afraid of you when I first met you because you know so much more, but I'm really glad I got to know you."

"What are you going to tell the kids?"

"The truth, I guess, about what I did. I don't want them to feel guilty though. I always felt guilty because my parents were unhappy and my father was disappointed in me. I don't want that to happen to them. I'll have to try to find some way. Al will dump it on them if he gets a chance. He thinks they should be more disciplined, whatever that means."

A nurse came into the room.

"Visiting hours are over now, I'm afraid."

"So soon?"

Jennifer nodded to the nurse, and she left the room. She was very young, and she seemed out of place in the middle of all this.

"I'll come over tomorrow sometime," Jennifer said.

"Thanks for coming. I'm sorry to pour it all out on you."

"I don't mind," Jennifer said. "I hope it makes you feel better."

"How are things with you?"

"Not bad. A bit chaotic. Is there anything you want?"

"Not unless you can think of a book that will make me feel that this is all worthwhile and significant."

"How about the Bible?"

Barbara gave a little snort of laughter.

"I don't think I've read it since I got gold stars for memorizing verses."

Jennifer hugged her friend and walked to the door of the room. As she turned to wave, the distance between them was suddenly exaggerated; the night outside the window seemed to invade and wrap itself around Barbara's shoulders, making her figure look smaller, the thin legs poignant and vulnerable. Jennifer couldn't conquer the distance. She was like a lost spaceship in the spreading darkness of the universe. She turned and walked away from the door, down the wide echoing hall and past the nursing-station to the elevator. The bright white uniforms of the nurses seemed like costumes.

As Jennifer walked out the front door of the hospital, she heard a voice beside her.

"Excuse me."

It was the man she had seen getting out of the elevator. Under the cap of dark curling hair, his glasses reflected the streetlights. His eyes held her.

"Is she all right?"

"Who do you mean?"

"Barbara. You're Jennifer Mallen, aren't you? Her friend?"

"Yes."

"I'm Tom Van Every. I've seen you, but I don't think we've ever met."

He held out his hand to her. She shook hands. It was less absurd than she would have thought. There was something comfortable and familiar about him.

"She wouldn't see me," he said.

He seemed to assume that Jennifer would understand.

"She seems all right," Jennifer said. "I don't think she'll try again."

"Thank you," he said. He turned and walked away, moving quickly, his arms swinging a little in an almost military way. Tom Van Every. She knew of him as a judge in the provincial court, but she had never realized the name went with the face that moved through various backgrounds of her time in Kingston. He was an attractive man; she could see how Barbara had fallen for him.

She stood for a moment on the hospital steps, watching the man walk away in the cool September darkness. The hospital was a vantage point, one of the vital organs of the living body of the night city, like a heart that beat faithfully through the hours of the body's sleep.

Eugene was out there in the city, unless he'd had the sense to go back to the hospital. She went down the steps and turned toward home, trying not to anticipate a scene with Robert. It was more and more impossible to talk to him. Everything seemed edged with steel. Would he ever find a woman to make him happy? He seemed to have no patience with the kind of straightforward woman who might be able to give him peace. He was fascinated by destruction and difficulty, seeking some fierce edge of awareness. Addicted to pain and loss. Perhaps it was a kind of honesty, certainly there was a hard fire about it. She thought of him with an interest and respect that was almost a kind of love, but she couldn't bear to be near him. In a few more years the children would be grown up, and she would never have to see him again.

His car was parked in front of the house, the wheels up on the pavement to indicate to her as she arrived that he had been hurried and upset, not taken time to park properly before running in to rescue his children.

The door of the house was locked. She took out her key, but as she reached toward it, it was drawn away from her, and Robert towered over her, waiting. Jennifer remembered once telling a friend that there was no hope for a couple with such an insane difference in height.

"Did Eugene come back?" she said. Might as well confront it directly.

"Is that his name, this madman you have hanging around?"

"Did he come back?"

"I didn't see him. He may be lurking in the garden waiting for me to leave."

"He's just a boy."

"Scared Cindy out of her wits. Gavin was all set to go out looking for him with a kitchen knife. It seems an odd time to go out."

"I got him out of the house first."

"And left him screaming on the porch. Why did you have to go so urgently?"

Jennifer wanted to say nothing, to refuse. He had no right to ask. But he did, dammit, they were his children.

"I had to go to the hospital. I promised Barbara . . . she tried to kill herself this morning. I promised I'd see her."

"You could have waited a few more minutes."

"I told her I'd be there by the end of visiting hours."

"I expect they'd have let you in later on."

"Well he didn't come back, so there's no problem."

"He hasn't come back yet."

"I can handle him."

"Can you? Cindy said he knocked you down."

"I tripped on the phone cord. And besides I didn't have time to convince him of anything. I just had to get him out."

"Do you have many patients coming around here? If you're going to be a mother figure to the psychiatric hospital, maybe the kids should live with me."

"Don't be ridiculous. I don't work with disturbed patients. He's just someone I happened to meet. I didn't invite him here. Any other time I could have talked him into going back to the hospital."

"Always in control."

Jennifer could feel herself retreating from him. There was no point in trying to communicate. He didn't want to touch her. He wanted another failure, another little edge of fire.

"Do you want a cup of coffee while you're here?" she said.

"I helped myself to a glass of milk. I thought perhaps you could spare me that."

"Of course."

"How is Barbara?"

"She'll get over it, I think. As much as people ever get over anything. She's not going to become a happy woman all of a sudden, but . . . I don't know. I think it was just circumstance."

"Al got a new woman?"

"A lot of things."

"She should have left him years ago."

"Simple solution."

"Simple problem. A beautiful woman like that could surely make a life for herself. Unless she's addicted to agony. She looks a bit as if she might be. Those wonderful bones showing through the skin as if she starved herself."

"She eats quite well. I've seen her."

"There's no need to be literal-minded." He reached for

22

his coat. "I'd better go. Keep the door locked eh?"

Robert stood by the door. His hand was clenched over his solar plexus; his stomach must be bad again.

"Have you gone to a doctor?"

"He'd tell me to relax. Not the most useful advice in the world."

He let himself out. Jennifer locked the door behind him.

"Gavin," she shouted, "are you in bed?"

"Not quite."

"What does that mean?"

"It means I'm not."

Jennifer made her way up the stairs and into Gavin's room. He was sitting in the corner of the room with a pile of comic-books around him.

"In you go."

"Dad's going to take me to the Museum of Science and Technology in Ottawa."

"Sounds like fun."

She stroked his head. It wouldn't be long, she suspected, till he found such gestures of affection embarrassing. He would begin to mature, and their whole relationship would change shape. She bent and kissed his cheek.

"Good night, sweet prince."

Jennifer made her way downstairs. She could hear Cindy splashing in the bathtub. Jennifer sat down in a comfortable chair and stared at the living-room wall. Had Eugene gone back to the hospital yet or was he roaming the darkness?

Cindy came down the stairs in her pyjamas. She stuck her head round the corner.

"You want some hot chocolate? I'm making some."

"No thanks, Cindy. I'll maybe have something later on."

As soon as the words were out, she regretted them. It wasn't often that Cindy made such an offer; it was important that she be allowed to take on an adult role.

"Changed my mind," Jennifer said, loud enough for Cindy to hear in the kitchen. "I'd like a cup."

"Okay."

Jennifer decided to read something familiar and comfortable, *Middlemarch* perhaps, for the third or fourth time. Each time she read the book again, she found that she read again her own character at the times of the previous readings, always with a sense of shock, a terrifying sense of the callowness of her understanding. Why didn't I see that ten years ago? Of course one never did, never could. The last time she had read it, she had been disappointed in the ending, Dorothea's ambition settling down into wifely duty toward Will Ladislaw. It had seemed a cheat.

Cindy brought her the hot chocolate. She was taller than Jennifer now and as she reached sexual maturity had begun to develop an unexpected elegance. Jennifer found it mysterious, almost resented the alien gift. Cindy was 'feminine,' that strange exotic desirable thing that Jennifer had never been.

"Are you going to bed now?" Jennifer said.

"I'm going to drink this and read for a while."

"Want me to come and tuck you in?"

"Not especially."

"See you in the morning."

"Are you mad because I phoned Daddy?"

"No. It was a sensible thing to do. I should have thought of it."

"Will that guy be coming back?"

"I hope not. He seems a bit desperate. I guess he needs all the help he can get."

"Is he part of your job?"

"No."

Cindy sounded like Robert, simplifying, detached.

"But we're responsible for other things in life besides our jobs."

Cindy just looked at her and walked out of the room. The scent of hostility was left behind. Jennifer wanted to take the hot chocolate out to the kitchen and dump it, but that was childish, getting revenge on a thirteen-year-old. She sipped the hot sweet drink, and when she finished, she took the cup to the kitchen and rinsed it. She found Bena up on the counter, captured her and put her out for the night. While she was on her feet, she got herself *Middlemarch*.

Jennifer had first read the book for a third-year university course. How patronizing she had been that time about Dorothea's naive inability to understand her own sexual needs. Jennifer had been full of an adolescent delight in her own sexual awakening. It was during her own early days with Robert, and everything was part of the intoxication of this tall confident moody boy who came from Toronto and seemed years more sophisticated than Jennifer.

Jennifer read until bedtime. Now and then Eugene or Barbara would come back to her mind, but there was so clearly nothing she could do for them. Nothing sensible. She could hear Robert's voice, icy and sarcastic. "You're always so sensible." Well, she was, and no longer felt apologetic about it. She was herself and need no longer try to please him by being intense. He could have that, burn away in his little apartment with his young lovers.

Jennifer turned off the lights, checked to make sure that all the doors were locked and went up to bed. It was nearly time for her period to start, and her breasts were heavy and tender, so she left on the brassière under her long nightgown. She would sleep better. As she lifted the white bedspread, she thought of the Robert Louis Stevenson poem called "The Land of Counterpane." She sat on the bed and took down her hair, feeling like a sick and pampered child of the eighteen-nineties, then brushed out her hair and braided it for sleep. She picked up the book from the table beside her.

There was a pleasant loneliness about going to bed by herself, a lack of tension or expectation. She hadn't had a man for months, and the last one had worked out badly enough that she didn't half mind. Probably she was ready to live the rest of her life alone. The idea was almost comforting.

The last time she had made love to Robert was the night he had wakened her at four in the morning terrified that his young mistress had killed herself. As it turned out, she had simply run off to England to escape him. Poor Robert. That night Jennifer had felt sorry for him and yet been angry and distant. She felt badly about it now, but there had been no alternative. Solitude had been growing in her even then. She put down the book, turned out the light and snuggled under the covers. Once it had been very different; she had wanted nothing but to touch him. How had she changed so much?

There was a Sunday night, the last of the Hart House concerts before the Christmas holidays. In a few days she'd be going back home for Christmas. The thought of parting from Robert had given the evening a kind of poignancy that made her more uneasy than usual, though she was always tense with him, tongue-tied, abrupt, yet wanting to be with him, excited by his energy and knowledge.

She had met him in an English class. He didn't speak in class especially often, but when he did his remarks seemed to be well informed and curiously impassioned. A wit in one of her classes said Robert always made him think of the cartoon in which a Victorian young lady is staring at a Victorian young man and asking "Are you intense?"

One day after class, Jennifer found herself having coffee with a group of people that included Robert, and that evening he phoned to ask her out. He seemed nervous on the phone, and she was surprised that he should be so simply human. His manner in class made him seem beyond such things.

By the night of the concert, they had gone out several times, begun to have long, almost painful goodnight kisses at the door of her residence.

The music they heard that night was startling for her. It was Healey Willan's choir, and she had never heard any-

26

thing like it. Jennifer wasn't unmusical, had sung alto in a church choir that stuck to hymns in traditional harmony, but the only music she knew was what she had learned at school or heard in church, that and the few recordings her friends played in residence. The intricate counterpoint of this choir was a new world. It gave her a sudden glimpse of unheard-of spiritual possibilities. She wanted to say something about it to Robert, but she was afraid he would think her naive. She hated seeming like a smalltown girl.

At the end of the concert, they made their way silently out through the crowd. The air was sharp and cold, and a few flakes of snow were falling. Jennifer felt that it was perfect, everything was.

"Let's walk," Robert said.

"Sure."

They went around the circle of Queen's Park. Through the darkness, they could see the wooden bandstand, remnant of musical summers in the past. The world was all space, the snowflakes a punctuation of the immense darkness.

They walked once around the park and turned back toward Jennifer's residence. As they walked along a dark passage, Robert turned toward Jennifer, taking her in his arms and pushing her back against the wall. She was almost frightened at being handled and moved like this, yet pleased as well with the sense of not being in her own power. He bent down to kiss her, and as they kissed, his hand reached into her coat and took hold of her breast. She tried to draw away because it was what she had always done, but she was held against the wall, and there was no place to move to.

Robert stepped back from her and unfastened her coat. His hands moved over her breasts and down over her belly. She closed her eyes, wanted to cry, not that she was frightened now, but simply that what she felt was powerful and autonomous, out of her control. They clung together. She hugged him savagely, eager to sense the shape of this thin bony tall body. He kissed her ears and her hair. His arms were dragging her down toward the ground, but she wouldn't go, not here on the pavement, she pulled away and walked into the quadrangle. She stood still in the few flakes of snow. He walked up and stood beside her.

"There's no place else to go," he said.

He had known what she was feeling. She turned and seized him and held him tight.

Jennifer lay in the dark of her bed and found that she was aroused by the memory of that night. And yet she didn't want Robert now or ever. He was not the same now, nor she.

2

As usual, the room was too hot. It was in the basement, and there was no ventilation, in fact the room had been used for storage until Jennifer had begun the symbol project. Sometimes they worked with the door open, but there was a constant progression of orderlies and patients going by, and it was hard enough for the children to concentrate without that. In the last few minutes, Melinda had started rolling her head as she did when she was distracted, and Jeffrey was making his noises.

All four of the children in her group were classified as retarded, but since they had varying physical handicaps and were apparently unable to speak it was difficult to estimate their mental abilities. That was the point of the symbol program, the reason Jennifer had been able to develop it.

The previous year she had run across an article in *Time* about the use of the symbolic language of Charles Bliss at the Centre for Crippled Children in Toronto. Bliss, an Austrian Jew who had survived a concentration camp, had invented a system of visual symbols to serve as a clear and incorruptible language of international communication. The man himself was obviously one of those fascinating cranks, an eccentric idealist riding a hobby-horse into the dark night of history, but through an accident a teacher of crippled children had come on his system and found it perfect for such speechless children as those with cerebral palsy.

At the time Jennifer read the article, she had made tentative arrangements to return to her part-time job at one of the local high schools, but she wasn't excited about it. They wouldn't take her on full-time since she had no teaching certificate, though she had teaching experience in one of the rougher secondary-modern schools in South London. Apart from that she found the work predictable; the students were neither good enough nor bad enough to make it a challenge. She had already begun to spend some time at the mental hospital as a volunteer working with retarded children, and when she read the article in *Time* she wrote to Toronto and got more information about the symbols and approached David McAdam, the head of the children's unit, about the possibility of starting a symbol project with the retarded children.

Many of those working in the hospital suspected that some of the children were potentially brighter than could be proved by tests, though shut off by handicaps that prevented communication. It wasn't many years since children with cerebral palsy were assumed to have no significant intelligence. The symbols, starting with simple concepts but offering many possible elaborations, and requiring pointing rather than speech, might make it possible to reach more of the children. McAdam, whose research was in psychometrics, was skeptical of projects that cast doubt on the standard tests, but by suggesting it as a research project, and with the support of Irving Kilborg, the head of social work, Jennifer had managed to get a pilot project started.

Mornings and afternoons on alternate days, she met her four children in this stuffy basement room and tried to pull them out of their silence and into the world. The four were arranged in a semi-circle around her, Melinda and Rennie, Jeffrey and George. Melinda and Jeffrey were in wheelchairs, the other two could sit on their own. The room had no windows and was painted the depressing cream and green of most institutions. At first, since it was meant to be only a temporary location, Jennifer hadn't bothered adding any colour or decoration, but it seemed now there was little likelihood of moving anywhere else.

Melinda was her star pupil.

"Why aren't we comfortable in this room, Melinda?"

The rolling head was brought under some control, and her hand began to move toward the symbol board. The hand was permanently clenched, and she did her pointing with the outside knuckle. At first Jennifer had found it too slow and painful to watch her hand struggle toward one of the symbols, had wanted to help her, to say the words herself, not to have to wait, but as they went on with their work, her patience had increased.

Most of those in the hospital believed Melinda to be not far below normal intelligence, though suffering from cerebral palsy and perhaps other brain damage. She didn't belong here, and the hospital social workers were trying to convince her mother to take her home, but the mother was resisting. She had managed to find some doctor to diagnose the child as hopelessly retarded, and she clung to that. The father had vanished years before.

Jennifer and Irving Kilborg were planning to give Melinda's mother a demonstration of her daughter's ability to think and communicate, using the symbols. If they could force the woman to communicate with Melinda, it might have some effect.

Melinda's knuckle had stopped at the three-sided box, the symbol for *room*. It started to move again, then fell away from the board and struggled back up. For this child, a sentence took all the heroism of a voyage to the North

Pole. The hand moved. Jeffrey's noises were getting louder.

Melinda's hand crawled on its tense and indirect path across the board. The knuckle rested on the symbol for *hot*.

"Yes, Melinda, the room *is* hot. How do you feel when the room is hot?"

The hand picked out the words. *I, want, water.*

"All right. I'll get you a drink in just a minute, Melinda."

Jennifer turned to Rennie and George.

"Melinda says the room is hot." She drew the curving line with its three darts on the moveable blackboard in front of them. Rennie focused her eyes on it and put her fingers in her mouth to pull at her lip. George appeared to be looking the other way. His hand was rubbing his penis. Did he need to urinate? Jennifer wondered. Or was it just nervousness that made him do it?

She pointed to the symbol on the board and repeated the word. She took Rennie's hand and walked with her to the wall where the heating-pipes passed through. They were insulated, but the heat could be felt through the insulation. She took Rennie's hand and held it close to the pipe.

"Hot," she said, then placed Rennie's hand on a card with the symbol on it and repeated the word.

She went through the same procedure with George. He smiled happily. He was always pleased at attention and movement, but it wasn't clear that he was ever going to catch on to the symbols.

"I'll go and get Melinda's drink now."

She left a couple of favourite toys on George's table to keep him distracted and went down the hall to a small canteen. Each time she moved through the corridors of the institution today, she expected to meet Eugene, find him lying in wait for her, but he hadn't appeared. Maybe he was embarrassed about last night.

She took the water to Melinda. Should she have brought some for the others? Perhaps not. Let them see the benefits of communicating. The afternoon session was nearly

31

over. She had left the door open for the last few minutes to cool the room. A slow parade of retarded men was going past. Rennie's eyes followed their movement.

"What do you see, Rennie?"

Rennie made some cheerful noises that indicated she might know the answer, but she didn't move her hand. Jennifer moved her finger to the symbol for man.

"You see a man."

She stroked Rennie's head. All the children liked to be touched, but to Rennie it was especially important. Often she would catch hold of Jennifer's clothing and hold tightly to it. She needed the constant reassurance of physical contact.

Jeffrey's noises had begun again. Jennifer turned to him. Some days she found it hard to face him. He was monstrously ugly, and, so far as anyone could tell, hopelessly retarded. His body was distorted, and his face formed of bones that were unbalanced and grotesque, a lump on one side of the forehead, a jaw that appeared to be shrivelled. It looked like a Hallowe'en mask. His head twitched and rolled constantly. Yet a couple of the therapists were sure there was something there, and Jennifer was inclined to agree. McAdam thought he was hopeless, and even Irving was skeptical, but Jennifer swore there were moments when something flashed through the eyes and over the features of the face, some kind of comprehension.

An old man came wandering in the door and stood for a moment. No orderly came to lead him out.

"Man," Jennifer said, pointing to the card on Jeffrey's table. "Man."

Jeffrey's noises began. They were both hollow and guttural, coming from somewhere in his chest. Had they changed in quality just now? Was there some glimmer of understanding there? The head lolled, and she thought for a moment one of the eyes was looking up toward her from under the hunch of the shoulder. She tried to hold his look.

32

The head moved down, the contact (if there had been any contact) was broken. The man at the door had stood perfectly still until now, puzzled by this new place, perhaps lost, forgetting how he had come here.

He looked toward Rennie and smiled, made his way toward her. Jennifer stepped toward Rennie's chair. They were harmless enough, these men, but now and then one would get excited or upset. The man made a noise and reached out to one of the symbols in front of Rennie.

"Puhjuh," he said.

"Yes," Jennifer said. "It's a picture."

The symbol was taped to the board. He tried to pull it loose.

"No," Jennifer said. "You can't have it."

His face looked puzzled, then abruptly he seemed to forget it and turned to leave the room. An orderly met him at the door.

"Get out here, Fred," the orderly said, pulling him by the shoulder. "You stay in line."

The old man and the orderly vanished. The moment was over. Moments came and went like that in here. There were two time scales, the single moment and eternity. Because the patients couldn't remember or couldn't hold things together, there was always the possibility of a dramatic moment when who-knows-what flower of chaos might suddenly bloom. Yet ultimately the place was changeless. The human jetsam found here was seldom capable of significant change or development. Each was trapped in a dim eternity of repeated gestures.

"The orderly will be coming for you soon, Melinda. What will you do then?"

The hand slowly moved, the tongue hanging loose with the effort of concentration to bring the knuckle to the symbol.

"You're going to watch television. Anything else?"

The hand crawled forward.

33

I, want, food.

"You're hungry. So after television you'll have supper. How will that make you feel?"

Funny.

"You're teasing me again Melinda."

There was a glitter of laughter in the child's eyes, and Jennifer bent to hug her. Two orderlies appeared at the door. It was time for the children to leave.

"Time to go now. Goodbye Melinda."

The hand moved to the symbol for goodbye. Once again, as Jeffrey's head lolled, she thought he was looking up and she tried to meet his glance, but once again the head moved away.

"We'll keep trying, Jeffrey," she said. "One of these days you'll catch on."

The noises began. Were they simply a companionable response or was he answering? Why was she so convinced that Jeffrey was responding to her? McAdam and Irving weren't fools. But there was intelligence there, feeling. If she did nothing else in her life, it was worth the struggle to try to break through the wall of silence to reach him.

Jennifer left the room and walked up the stairs to the main floor where she had left her jacket in the staff-room. In the basement there were no windows, and it was a shock now to look out and see the grey September afternoon. It looked cold, and she regretted bringing her bike. Once again she thought that perhaps she should buy a small car, but she could never quite convince herself that it was a necessary expense. When she and Robert were divorced he had taken the car, since he had always done most of the driving. Now and then Jennifer wondered if refusing to buy a car was some obscure way of punishing Robert. Perhaps.

She met Irving in the staff-room. He looked tired, and that was unusual for Irving.

"Have you talked to Melinda's mother again?" she said.

"Not yet. Haven't been in the mood for hysteria."

34

"You look tired. What's the matter?"

"Sick kids. Deborah's got some kind of intestinal thing that won't go away. I was up half the night with her. And Joey's allergy is worse so we have to get rid of the cat, and David says if the cat goes, he goes."

"Poor Irving."

"It's a father's lot. The only thing worse is to be a mother. Now I know why my mother was the way she was."

Jennifer put on her jacket. The sky was darkening, and it looked as if it might rain before she got home.

"What's this I hear about Barb Walker?" Irving said.

"What did you hear?"

"That she slashed up."

"It's true, but she's trying to keep it quiet."

"That husband of hers. I'm surprised she didn't do it years ago."

"I never took you for a moralist."

"I'm not a moralist. He's got no class."

"Are you going to see Melinda's mother soon?"

"Don't be in a hurry. With Melinda gone, who knows if McAdam will continue the class?"

"What do you mean?"

"He doesn't think any of the others are worth the trouble."

"I think Rennie's learning something."

"Maybe, but who can afford a class for one kid?"

"Melinda doesn't belong in here," she said. "I'll worry about the class later on."

Jennifer walked down the long blank corridor and out the door. As she went out, she saw a police car parked on the other side of the quadrangle. Someone must have wandered downtown and got lost.

Did Eugene ever come back or did he set off for Ottawa? She should have asked someone about him. She unlocked her bike. On the way home, the wind was blowing from the east into her face. It made pedaling an effort.

The house was empty when she walked in, the children not yet home, and Jennifer wandered around for a few moments, trying unsuccessfully to fill it with her own presence. She sat down in a chair in the living-room, suddenly and inexplicably frightened by the loneliness of the place. The empty spaces of the universe seemed to echo the emptiness inside her, and she felt a moment of childish panic. Her mind was like an instrument sending out radar waves, but none were bounced back and recorded. The screen was blank. Would it be like this forever? The children would come home, but they were only a temporary shelter. They only postponed the bad time. And friends? She had some, had none. Irving was a good warm presence, but his life was used up by others. Barbara needed her, but there was no real intimacy. Jennifer revealed nothing of herself. Intimate friendships between women were the fashion these days, but Jennifer had been born too soon for that or too late.

The radar sent out its waves; nothing returned. The screen was empty.

Jennifer went to the kitchen and took out a chicken pie that she'd frozen on the weekend and put it in the oven to cook. She opened a beer. Right after supper she must walk down to the hospital and see Barbara; she ought to take her something. Since there was no time to go downtown, she'd stop at the corner store and get a paperback or some magazines.

The man who stopped her at the hospital doorway, how did he know she was there to see Barbara? Barbara must have spoken of her; he must know her face from concerts and parties they had both attended. It was uncomfortable to feel herself known, recognized, discussed by this man she had never met. Everyone's world was like that, circles that intersected other circles, and it was especially true in a small city like Kingston, she had always recognized that, yet at the moment of discovering a new intersection there was always a moment of surprise.

She remembered when she and Robert had first moved to England, one afternoon walking through the Tate Gallery with an English friend, they had met three different people they knew from Toronto. Once you established the framework of your life, your world became smaller, more open to odd collisions. And the mobility and centralization, of contemporary life made the coincidences more likely. All travellers to Timbuctoo will meet in Timbuctoo.

The door slammed, and Cindy walked in and straight up the stairs to her room. She was growing moodier by the day. Jennifer wondered whether she ought to go up and see her but decided to leave her alone. Children that age needed privacy. She'd come down when she was ready.

When Jennifer was thirteen, she had got her privacy on long walks. With her mother and her young brother in the small house, it always seemed crowded, though there was more space after Harold went overseas. Jennifer would go off down McNab's Road, past the silent farm fields, her hands in her coat pockets, immersed in fantasies, making up who she was by inventing stories for herself. She would go to the city and become a musician, an actress, something marvellous. She would go to the city and disaster would befall her, and she would die in circumstances of high drama. She would go to the city and be famous for something. All of the stories began with the same trip to the city, Toronto, of all places, that stodgy city of churches where, in those dreary days of the nineteen-forties, you could shoot a cannon down Yonge Street on Sunday and endanger no-one. This was her city of light. And her eventual journey there took the blandest and most predictable of forms; she went to university because she was the brightest girl in the school, and her parents were willing to sacrifice.

For Robert, born and raised there, Toronto could never be the city of light. He was exploding with the need to escape, so right after their marriage, they went to England, settling in London and living on the fringes of the world of

37

books and publishing, involved in the CND, the Labour Party, all the good causes.

Gavin came in and threw his coat on a hall chair.

"Hang it up, please."

"Oh Mum, don't be a fussbudget."

"It's a mother's privilege. Where have you been?"

"Jeg and I were playing floor-hockey. I was gonna invite him for supper, but I figured I better not. Because of his mother. I figured they should all be at home."

What an odd sense of propriety the boy had.

"What's for supper?" he said.

"Chicken pie."

"I guess it's better than nothing."

"I hope so."

"*Get Smart*'s on."

"It'll be ready in half an hour."

Gavin made his way out. Jennifer was nearly finished her beer and wondered about having another. She should make some effort not to put on too much weight. It was unhealthy. She had a responsibility to her body.

After making a salad, Jennifer said farewell to her good intentions and opened another beer. Life was a fatal disease no matter how you lived it. From downstairs she could hear the noise of the TV. Gavin was a bit of an addict, and she worried about the consequences, not that she expected him to become suddenly violent, but rather that the constant high level of stimulation must have some bad effect on the nervous system. A whole society chronically over-stimulated couldn't be healthy. Perhaps she was just falling into the mistake of wanting to inflict her own quiet country childhood on the whole world.

When Jennifer called the children for supper, Cindy came down looking angry and depressed.

"What's wrong?"

"That stupid Miss Lawton. She hates me. Someone passed me a note, and I got the blame for it."

38

"Probably other times, you've escaped the blame for things you have done."

"You would say that. You really hate me, don't you?"

"Don't be silly."

"Stupid Gavin never does anything wrong."

Gavin was staring down at his plate.

"But Mother, I don't like my sister," he said in a high voice and replied in a deep one, "Shut up and eat."

"Don't be any stupider than you have to," Cindy said.

"Cut it out, you two. I'm not in the mood for sibling rivalry." She took a sip of her beer.

"How many bottles of beer did you have tonight?" Cindy said.

"None of your business."

"Too many."

"Just eat your supper."

A sulky silence descended on the table.

"Can you help me make those buns tonight?" Cindy said. It was a peace offering.

"I have to go to the hospital for a while. Maybe I can later on."

"Is that crazy guy going to come back here?" Gavin said.

"I don't think he'll be coming back. But I'll lock the door when I go out."

"How long's Mrs. Walker going to be in the hospital?" Cindy said.

"I don't know."

They finished eating, and Cindy stood up silently and walked from the room. Gavin drank his milk and looked up.

"What's for dessert?"

"Nothing special. Want some ice cream?"

"Any maple walnut?"

"Yup."

"I'll have that."

Jennifer could hear Cindy talking on the upstairs phone. She hoped the phone call would put her in a better mood.

She gave Gavin his ice cream and was making herself coffee when Cindy appeared from upstairs with her coat on.

"I'm going over to Daddy's apartment."

Jennifer was angry, but she controlled her voice.

"I want you to stay here with Gavin."

"Gavin can stay by himself."

"I don't want him to stay here by himself."

"I told Daddy you were going out and he said I could come over there if I wanted."

Jennifer and the girl were facing each other. Cindy was already a shade taller than Jennifer, and Jennifer was surprised to find herself resenting this, wanting to hit her. The anger shocked her. It was like what she had sometimes felt with Robert, perhaps because Robert was involved. She couldn't bear this taking sides.

"Take Gavin with you."

"I don't want to take Gavin. He wasn't invited."

"I'm sure Gavin's as welcome there as you are."

"Well, he's not coming."

"He is if I say so."

"It's all right," Gavin said. "I want to stay here. Jeg says he's going to phone me about some math homework."

"He can come if he wants," Cindy said sulkily. "I just don't want to be here if that creep comes back."

"I'm sure he won't."

It was perfectly justifiable in Cindy to be frightened of Eugene, and it was Jennifer's fault that he had come, that he had known where to find them. When he talked to her at the hospital, he just seemed an unhappy boy who needed help.

"Can I go now?" Cindy said.

"I suppose if you're going, there's no point standing around here with your coat on."

She should have realized that a woman alone with two children had to be aware of the dangers of her situation. When the door closed behind Cindy, she turned to Gavin.

"Will you be all right? I could phone Barbara and tell her I can't come."

"I'm not afraid of him."

"I don't think he'll turn up, but keep the door locked anyway."

"Sure."

He started down the stairs.

"And don't try to do your homework with the television set on."

"I can concentrate better that way."

"And pigs can fly too."

On the way to the hospital, Jennifer stopped at the corner store and bought some magazines. Bill, the little bald man who ran the store, short-changed her as usual, and she pointed it out and collected the proper change. She had the impression that Bill did it less out of greed than out of a desire to play games with the customers, see how many of them noticed. Once or twice she'd seen him give someone too much change.

When she walked into Barbara's room, she found her once again sitting in the chair beside the bed, but today she had on a dressing gown and makeup. Except for the bandages on her wrists, she looked once again the ideal wife and mother, as if she had achieved the perfect family size and (as Gavin had said) had come in to have her tubes tied.

"You look great," Jennifer said.

"I figured it was time to get myself fixed up a bit. I talked to a psychiatrist today, for the first time in my life."

"Was he helpful?"

"He said that cutting my wrists was a way of taking a holiday from personal responsibility, and that I had a perfect right to it." She looked down at the bandages. "It's still pretty embarrassing."

"While I was on the way out of here last night, a man stopped me and asked about you. Tom Van Every."

A slight wince moved over Barbara's fine features.

"What did he say?"

"He said that you wouldn't see him and asked if you were all right."

"He's really very nice. It's not his fault. I shouldn't have been so stupid."

"Nothing's that one-sided."

Barbara sat still, picking at the bandages. On her fingernails she had a pale frosted pink nail-polish that matched her lipstick.

"I wish . . ." She was silent.

"What?"

"I don't know. Something."

"Will you see him again?"

"He doesn't think we should. That's what made me do it. He doesn't want to get involved."

The cold bastard. Odd to try and put Barbara's words together with the man's face as she had seen it last night. The way he'd treated Barbara made Jennifer angry and spiteful toward him, yet her immediate response to him had been warm and positive. One always projected good qualities onto a handsome face.

"What I've got with Al is all right. We have a nice home. Mostly I don't mind the other women. What I mind more is that he doesn't know how to talk to me. We have to avoid being alone together. The kids are very useful for that, one of the advantages of a big family."

"I think maybe every marriage goes through that. Some come out the other side, some don't."

"Yours didn't."

"No." She didn't want to talk about it.

"Do you mind, now it's all over? I guess not. You're so strong willed."

"Sometimes it's lonely and bad, but then I see Robert and remember what it was like, and I'm glad it's over."

"I couldn't get along without Al."

"Comes of marrying young. You never had a chance to

42

grow up."

"Can I tell you something, Jenny? When I go to concerts at the kids' school, I sometimes feel as if I was still one of the pupils. The teachers all scare me, but I try not to let on."

Jennifer looked at the beautiful, well-groomed woman, thought of her home, decorated as if out of a magazine, full of the green of healthy, full-foliaged plants. All this created by someone who admitted to feeling like a frightened child.

"He's still the sexiest man I've ever met."

"Al?"

Barbara nodded. Jennifer had no answer when she said things like that. She and Barbara didn't speak the same language. Barbara's hands stopped fidgeting and became still in her lap. It was a perfect pose.

"How are your kids?" she said.

"I had a fight with Cindy before I left, but I suppose they're fine."

"Has Jeg been at your house today? I bet Al's having a terrible time with all of them on his hands. I hope he isn't just farming them out."

"Gavin said he'd been playing floor-hockey with Jeg after school, but he went home for supper."

"Jeg's going to be an athlete like his father. He spends hours in the basement working out with Al's weights. When he and Allen get into fights, Jeg always wins. It's not very nice for Allen, losing to his younger brother."

She was still, the hands poised in her lap, but Jennifer could see that there were tears gathering in her eyes, the body held in control, but the sorrow within welling up in spite of it.

"They've got me full of Valium," Barbara said, "and it keeps doing strange things to me. All afternoon I was either crying or sleeping."

She looked toward Jennifer and squeezed her hand.

"Thanks, Jen, for everything."

"I haven't done much."

43

"Sure you have."

Barbara took her hand away and picked up one of the magazines. She flipped the pages.

"Hey, that looks interesting," she said. "An indoor herb garden. I could make room for that in the sunporch."

She had withdrawn again. It was inevitable. She couldn't go on as nakedly vulnerable as she had been on Jennifer's first visit. Probably it was a sign that she was getting herself back, regaining her role. It was one of the commonplaces of contemporary psychology that you could be permanently raw and naked. A whole slang of the previous decade had advertised this possibility, total spontaneity. Jennifer had tried to believe in it, but it had cost too much. Intimacy was occasional; beween the occasions, one drew back.

"When are you going home?" Jennifer said.

"Another couple of days. The doctor says I might as well take a couple of days' rest before starting in again."

"I remember once having a doctor who said he'd only been in hospital once but he'd loved it. Said it was better than a hotel because they brought the meals right to your bed."

"This is a pretty sad ward to be in. Two attempted suicides, a half-dozen menopausal depressions getting shock treatments. I'm not sure it's very restful."

"I suppose there's some benefit in being forced to sit and think."

"Maybe for you. You're a much stronger person than I am."

Why did people say these things to her? Because they wanted her to be strong, they assumed she was. She must have MOTHER painted on her forehead in letters of gold.

"Do you want me to drop round tomorrow?" Jennifer said.

"Sure, if you have the time, but I guess I don't really need it. I better get back into the habit of thinking about other people beside myself. I've had my little holiday."

Jennifer rose to go. Barbara walked to the door with her, and when they reached it, she put out her arms and hugged her.

Outside it was raining. The air was fresh and cool. As she walked home, she thought about Irving's remark about what might happen to her symbol class if Melinda went home.

Gavin came to the door to meet her. There had been no sign of Eugene. They watched television together for a while and then Jennifer sent him to bed and settled down with her book, her ear half-alert for the sound of a car door that would mean Robert had brought Cindy back. She read for half an hour but there was no sign of them. If Cindy was late to bed, she'd be crabbier than usual in the morning. Jennifer was a bit sleepy herself. She was almost dozing over the book when she was shocked awake by a knock at the door. She couldn't imagine who it might be at this hour. Please not Eugene. As she stepped to the door, she turned on the porch light so she could see who it was.

It was Tom Van Every. What was he doing here? She had nothing to say to him. She wanted to be left alone for a few hours to recover her energy for work in the morning.

Jennifer opened the door.

"Can I talk to you for a few minutes?" he said. "I'm sorry that it's late, but I've been driving around for an hour trying to decide whether to come here."

"It is late," Jennifer said. Damned if she'd make anything easy for him.

"I'll just be a few minutes."

She stood back and held the door. They stood awkwardly in the front hall, and something in Jennifer resisted making the obvious polite motion toward the living-room. She wanted to punish this smooth polite handsome man for his ability to hurt Barbara, even for the apparent gentleness of his manner. With an ill grace, she led him in and sat down facing him.

"I felt a need to explain myself," he said, plunging in. "Barbara won't see me, and that's probably best, but I'd like to talk it out with someone."

"Why me?" Jennifer said.

"Because you're Barbara's best friend. That's what she said."

She wasn't sure she wanted the responsibility of being Barbara's official best friend. Especially if it meant she was liable to visits like this. The thought seemed cruel, but tonight she was too far away to be kind.

"I've been explaining it over and over to myself, and I need to say it out loud, in front of somebody else, somebody who cares about Barbara."

"Go ahead then."

She felt a furious resistance to the look on his face, too damn sensitive as the self-justifying always were.

"I've been married for eleven years, and I've never been unfaithful to my wife."

"Do you expect me to find that noble?"

"It's just a fact."

"It would have been better for Barbara if you had gone to bed with her."

"I know that."

There was a pause. He seemed unable to speak.

"Go on and tell me."

"My marriage was a mistake. It's bad for me and probably bad for Eleanor. I made the mistake out of stupidity and unthinking complacency, but having made it, I worked hard at being responsible and living with it. I have the kind of personality you might expect in a judge. A deliberately upright man. Something of a prig at times."

Jennifer recognized the confession as meant to disarm hostility and refused to be disarmed.

"In the last year I've reached the end of something in myself. When I met Barbara through the nursery-school executive, it was the first time recently that I'd met a plea-

46

sant and attractive woman and been brought into contact with her in a natural way. I don't chase women at parties. Talking with Barbara was a great pleasure. We were on a committee together, and we met in perfect innocence for several months. It began to seem natural to talk on the phone or go out for coffee after meetings."

"Are you really that naive?" Jennifer said. She resented the ease with which he told the story.

"I am. Or I was. And was it really naive to think that here was a friend whose company was important to me? I realized suddenly that I didn't have many friends I could talk to." He said it so simply that she almost believed him, but it made her no less irritable. If he had done it all in stupid good faith, so much the worse.

"One day we were together, and I realized we couldn't just stay friends that way, that we both wanted more. So I went away and tried to think it through. Did I want, in the extreme case, to break up my marriage and hers?"

The easy flow of words again. Unfeeling bastard.

"You don't need to put on your courtroom manner for me," she said.

He stopped dead. For the first time he seemed really hurt by her hostility. Before it seemed something he was prepared to face so long as he could get the words out, get through his story.

"I'm sorry, but I suppose my courtroom manner, as you call it, has become second nature. Eleanor tells me I make speeches all the time."

He was silent now, looked to be on the point of leaving. He had got this far with his story, better to hear him out now. Let him get what satisfaction he could from the telling.

"It doesn't matter," she said. "Go on with what you were telling me."

"When I asked myself if I wanted to break up two marriages and make my life with Barbara, the answer was No,

I didn't. And short of that, I couldn't go on. I'm not good at lying. To myself or anyone else. It would have been all right for a while. I could have managed an affair for a few weeks as long as I was prepared for the truth to come out sometime, but I wasn't. I'm sure this all sounds very old-fashioned to you, but I told you what I'm like. In my personal and professional life, I have a strong loyalty to truth and fair-dealing. To the point of priggishness, or at least there are those who believe so."

"Yes, I can see they would," Jennifer said. It seemed an unfair comment, but it came out anyway.

"I don't mind that you say that. Now you know the facts, you can make whatever judgment you please. But at least you know my version of the facts, and that being the case, if Barbara wants to talk about it, you'll be better able to help her."

"Maybe."

"Thank you for listening. You didn't like it, but at least you let me finish." As he stood up to leave, Jennifer, for the first time, met his eyes and saw the real pain they held. Why did he have to spread his pain around? Let him keep it to himself.

She heard a car door outside. It must be Robert bringing Cindy back. She hoped he didn't decide to come in.

She and Van Every made their way to the door. The porch light was still on, and she could see two figures coming toward the house. Why had Robert chosen tonight to come in? He usually tried to avoid contact with her. Robert and Cindy arrived just as Van Every opened the door to leave.

"Don't let me drive anyone away," Robert said cheerfully. He sometimes took a malicious delight in awkward scenes.

"You're not. I was on my way."

Jennifer introduced the two men. Cindy slipped by into the house and upstairs.

"I know you by reputation," Robert said to the other

48

man, "as a judge who tempers mercy with justice."

He smiled as if it were a friendly remark.

"Nice to have met you," Van Every said. "Thank you again." This to Jennifer. He went away down the path. Jennifer held the door for Robert to come into the hall.

"Am I going to get ticked off for not being polite to him?"

"No."

Robert looked a bit puzzled at her response. Let him stay confused.

"Did you hear about your friend from the hospital?"

"Eugene?"

"He's been charged with rape."

"Oh no."

"I just heard it on the radio. After he left here last night, he broke into some girl's apartment up the street and gave her a pretty good going over."

"That's awful. Is the girl all right?"

"She's in the hospital."

"Poor thing."

"Are you still sure the kids are safe here?"

"Of course."

"You were sure last night too."

"Robert, it was a freakish thing. I don't work with disturbed patients. I met Eugene by accident. There's no danger to the children. But I'm glad you could come last night when Cindy phoned. I should have thought of it myself."

"I can understand why you didn't. In the same circumstances, I wouldn't have phoned you."

"Don't fret, Robert. I don't work with disturbed patients, and I have my hands full with my little group of hopeless cases."

"If you say so," he said and walked out the door. Jennifer stood and watched him drive away. She felt lonely and sad. What she should do, she decided, was to write a letter to her mother. It was quite a while since she'd heard from her.

3

October in sunlight: the earth was spinning at more than its usual speed today. There was too much of everything, too much colour, too much light, too much air in the lungs. Jennifer had wakened early, and as she lay there watching the shadows move across the ceiling had heard the wild cries of a flock of geese. They faded and died over the lake. It was an hour until the children needed to be up, but Jennifer got out of bed, dressed and went quietly downstairs and out. She got on her bike and began to ride through the deserted morning streets in sunlight under the yellow and scarlet and dark blood red of the trees. There had been rain during the night, and the leaves lay on the street in random patterns. She steered her bicycle through them as through a slalom.

Back at home, she made the children's breakfast, absurdly happy, on an edge that she almost feared losing, as if the speeding world might suddenly slow and crash. As she brushed Cindy's hair, the electricity in it lifted the little ends of broken hair away from her head. The light flickered on the streaks that were blonder than the rest.

"You have beautiful hair, Cindy."

"Does it look all right, really?"

"It's beautiful."

"I'm leaving now," Gavin said.

Jennifer reached out and hugged him, hard. He pulled away, half suffocated.

"I'm getting out of here before you wreck me."

Cindy walked away down the street, slowly, gracefully, the wind moving her hair.

Jennifer took her time riding to work, pedaling easily and letting her attention wander to the groups of children going to school, the line of cars moving downtown. She was moving against the flow of traffic, west along Union Street toward the mental hospital. She coasted down the long hill, feeling the giddy sense of speed again.

At the hospital, she locked her bike and made her way into the staff-room. David McAdam was there, making himself coffee. She was surprised at that; usually he sent his secretary, and there was a certain awkwardness to his movements that was deliberate, meant to suggest that he was not at ease with menial chores.

He was a tall man, balding, but with a young firm body. When he was younger, he'd been a competitive downhill skier, and now he kept himself in shape with running and cross-country skiing. He was a handsome man, yet unattractive, so clean that Jennifer felt he must be hiding a dirty soul.

"Good morning Jennifer."

The voice was surprisingly high-pitched and perhaps for that reason clipped and assertive to prevent any suggestion of effeminacy.

"Hello Dr. McAdam."

"How's the group progressing?"

"Fine, especially Melinda."

"That was to be expected."

"I think perhaps Rennic's close to catching on."

"You'll find the game isn't worth the candle with the others."

"I'm not ready to quit yet."

"Do your best, but don't expect miracles."

He put a lid on his coffee and turned to leave the room. He made Jennifer furious. She wanted to defeat him, to prove him wrong. Melinda's new ability to communicate was a miracle, but he denied it. It was to be expected.

Jennifer refilled the kettle and looked out the window toward the other wing. Eugene's wing. His preliminary hearing on the rape charge was tomorrow, and she was called as a witness. She had never been in court before, and she was nervous about what might happen. The prosecution planned to use her to establish that Eugene was in the neighbourhood and that he was in a disturbed state of mind. She didn't want to help them put Eugene in jail, but there seemed no alternative to going to court and answering their questions.

Past the corner of the building and between two trees, now almost bare, she could see the lake, sparkling blue in the sunshine. She tried to revive all she could of the morning's energy, to take it to her class. She'd force McAdam to reconsider. She'd prove to him the possibility of miracles. Those like McAdam who denied all possibilities prevented them from coming to pass.

She made her way down to the small classroom. She had decided to begin the symbols for the emotions, and on the table in the corner of the room was a pile of pictures she had clipped from magazines, faces with exaggerated expressions of happiness, sorrow, anger. While she waited for the orderlies to bring the children, she pinned the pictures to the cork board at the side of the room. Beside each one she fastened a large card with the appropriate symbol: happy, angry, afraid. All the symbols for feelings were variations on the valentine heart, with a rising arrow for happy, a falling arrow followed by a half-bracketed question-mark for afraid. Sometimes Jennifer found that she was translating the symbols in her own head in a poetic pidgin English: heart-rising, heart-falling, what-is-to-come?

Bill, one of the orderlies, stuck his head in the door.

"Hi there, Mrs. Mallen, you all ready for your kids?"

"Anytime, Bill."

"I'll bring them right down. That Jeffrey's a speed demon. He'd have me running with that chair till I had a heart-attack if I let him."

"Really?"

"He's a terror."

"How does he tell you that he wants to go fast?"

"He has his ways."

Bill withdrew his head and made off down the hall. If Jeffrey could communicate with him, there must be a way for Jennifer to reach him.

Bill came in leading George and Rennie, and behind him came another orderly pushing Melinda. There were plans to get Melinda an electronic chair soon so that she could make her own way around the hospital. The meeting with her mother had been a failure. The woman had been obdurate and hysterical in her refusal to communicate with the child. She insisted that Melinda belonged in an institution, that she had no responsibility for her.

"Good morning George," Jennifer said, bending to put her arm around his shoulders. "I'm going to put some symbols on your table. There's food. What did you have to eat this morning?" George smiled at her, but without making any apparent connection. "You had *food*," she said. "And here's *mouth*." She pointed to the circle and opened her own mouth in a circle and rounded it with her fingers, then put George's finger to his mouth, repeated the word and put his hand on the symbol. Again she opened her own mouth and put her finger on it.

"What am I pointing to?"

George's eyes flickered toward the table as if he had some idea what might be required of him, but he made no movement toward any of the symbols.

Jennifer put symbols on the tables in front of Rennie and Jeffrey. She put Melinda's symbol-board on her table, and they had a short conversation about simple things, sleep, breakfast, the day ahead. After a few minutes she went to the side wall where she had put up the symbols for the emotions. She worked through them out loud, trying to hold the attention of the four, to keep her own concentration at its peak so that her energy would lift them, push them ahead. She stood where she could catch Jeffrey's eye from time to time. Just let him see and listen, know he was included.

"Happy," she said. She mimed a large smile. "Bill says

53

that Jeffrey likes to go fast, that going fast makes Jeffrey *happy*."

Again she pointed to the symbol. Jeffrey began to make his noises. It was a response, she was sure of it. She placed the card for happy on his table.

"How do you feel when you go fast?"

The noises continued, but he made no movement toward the card. He had sufficient control of his hands to do it if he wanted to.

"How do you feel when Bill pushes your chair, and you go fast down the hall?"

He didn't move.

"Bill says it makes you happy."

She took Jeffrey's hand and moved it toward the card. He didn't want her to do it, and his noises got louder. She could have sworn he was fighting her, was furious. His hand tried to pull away. An idea struck her. Why not? She took the card with the symbol for angry and put it in front of him. His noises got louder again, his hand moved, and he put it down on the card.

Jennifer was exultant. She had reached him, this monster, this Caliban, he was a human being now with words for his feelings. Perhaps he understood everything she said. Had all along. She took a symbol from one of the other tables, the symbol for teacher.

"Who made you angry Jeffrey?"

Would he touch the symbol? Would he prove her right? She held her breath, waiting, the room quiet too, the other children still as if they knew the importance of it all. On the wall the faces, Happy, Angry, Sad, Afraid, watched like gods. Jennifer waited, urging him with all the love within her to reach out to that symbol.

His hand didn't move. Perhaps he didn't know that symbol. She picked up two or three others from the desks and spread them in front of him, formed questions that would allow him to use one or other of the symbols in his answer,

54

but there was no response, a quiet repetitive noise, the ugly unbalanced head hanging, the eyes avoiding her. She put the symbol for angry on his table. It was his now, he had conquered it. She tried to bring her attention back to the other children to continue the lesson, but it was difficult, she found her hands trembling.

"It was no accident," she said to Irving over lunch in the cafeteria. "He told me he was angry, then he just shut off, refused to communicate."

"As angry people do."

"Exactly."

"Had you spent much time working with that symbol?"

"I did a little introduction to the symbols for feelings, with pictures. Melinda's had that symbol for a while, but I doubt that she's used it often."

"So you think he's bright?"

"He's got some intelligence, but he's probably very disturbed. Why else pick out that word? And he was so fierce."

"So he's ugly, crippled and psychotic. I wonder what use intelligence is going to be to him?"

"You seem bitter today."

"It's Deborah."

"What's the trouble?"

"She keeps having intestinal problems. They've put her in the hospital for tests, but they can't seem to find out what's wrong."

"How long has she been in?"

"A couple of days. To tell you the truth, Jen, I'm scared. I'm afraid they'll never find it, and she'll die. Talk about hostages to fortune. . . . I don't know what I'd do. Curse God and live to spite him, I guess. I think Judy and I are both afraid of the same thing, but neither one of us will say it out loud. As if it would be bad luck."

"Is Judy Jewish?"

"No. Why."

"I've been meaning to ask for a long time and kept

forgetting."

"Does it matter?" There was an edge to his voice.

"Of course not. I was just curious, Irving. I thought I knew you well enough to ask without being self-conscious. What you said about cursing God sounded so Old Testament, it made me think of it."

Irving reached out and touched her hand.

"I'm sorry Jennifer. I'm jumpy today."

"Deborah seemed like a healthy kid the couple of times I met her."

"Never a sick day until this."

"I hope they find out what it is soon."

"Oh God, so do I. To visit her in the hospital would break your heart. All these sweet kids wandering around in pyjamas with big bandages from their operations."

"She'll be all right, Irving. I'm sure she will."

"It's nice to talk to you. You're always so serene."

Jennifer didn't recognize herself in what he said. Irving stood up.

"If you don't mind," he said, "I'm going to desert you now and make about 23 phone calls that I've been postponing."

He walked away from the table, and she watched him go, her heart going out to him in his fear for the life of his child. She remembered that fear from the time when Cindy was little and caught a series of throat infections with burning fevers. Eventually penicillin would kill the infection, the temperature would fall, but in the meantime there were those terrible nights of carrying Cindy through the darkness, holding her tightly to keep death away. The same thing when she had measles later on. She and Robert would take turns walking with her, and when they returned to each other couldn't speak or touch, as if they were too naked and any contact would burn the skin.

Jennifer left the cafeteria and walked toward the lake. There was wind now, but it was still clear, the air perfectly transparent as she looked across the rolling whitecaps toward Wolfe Island.

Tomorrow she would see Eugene in court. Her life seemed to have entered one of those periods when disaster fell on everyone around her. Barbara, Eugene, Irving: she was their witness. As she walked along the edge of the hospital grounds, the waves falling on the gravel beach beneath her, she reviewed the events with Jeffrey, sought a way of proceeding that would allow her to reach him again. She must remember to assume that he understood her. When she went back to the classroom, she made a series of notes on methods for reaching Jeffrey again. She spent most of the afternoon on it, went and saw him in the ward, talked to Bill and a couple of the other orderlies and therapists. They were all surprised that she expected to get anywhere with him. Jennifer began to feel depressed as the afternoon wore on. Maybe it was just an accident, something she had misunderstood, interpreted as she wished it to be. To cheer herself up, she went and put in some extra time working with Melinda. That was encouraging.

At the end of the day, Jennifer made her way out of the building alone. The staff moved around her in time with the life of the patients, the slow shuffle of the senile, the flat vacant faces of the retarded, the bored glances of the alcoholics, the evasions of the psychotic. All the drugged truants from the small struggles of normality moved in their patterns like sea creatures at the bottom of the ocean. Drowned in the pacific.

On the way home, Jennifer pedaled down King Street to the beer store. She wedged a pack of six bottles in the bag behind her seat and turned the bike toward home.

When she walked in, she heard a sound of hammering from the basement. She put her head over the stairs and shouted hello.

"Hello yourself," Gavin said cheerfully.

"What are you up to?"

"Fixing my table."

"Good."

The table beside Gavin's bed had been wobbling for months, but she had never seen him do any carpentry before, and Robert had left little in the way of tools and equipment. Still it was good that he was determined to be independent and do things on his own. It was too bad he'd never been able to meet his grandfather. The man's skill and knowledge had died with him. The only one who ever learned from him was her brother Harold. Gavin had asked about her father a couple of times and seemed interested that he had been a skilled cabinet-maker.

Jennifer thought of showing him the poem she had written, nearly twenty years ago now, on the plane coming back from England to her father's funeral. It was about her father's hands and was not a good poem, just one of those things you write in a moment of emotion, but she had read it once or twice since, and it still moved her. Maybe when Gavin was older she'd show it to him.

She put the beer in the fridge, except for one bottle which she opened. As she was opening it, Cindy arrived at the door with her friend Alice. She was a cheerful pretty girl who had a good effect on Cindy, and Jennifer was always glad to see her.

"Can Alice and I make supper?"

"Sure, if you want to."

"We're going to make spaghetti."

Cindy was looking, a little disapprovingly, at the glass of beer. Jennifer had never worked out why she disapproved, something to do with beer being an unladylike drink. Or that it made you fat. Sometime she would ask her, not that Cindy was likely to answer. She hated questions, saw them all as intrusions on her precarious independence.

Jennifer sipped her beer as Cindy and Alice laughed and collided in the kitchen. More hammering from the basement. At this moment, she felt relaxed and detached, pre-

58

siding over a storybook household, the children growing happily toward security and independence. The late-afternoon sunlight was catching the leaves at an angle, making them look as if they were lit from within.

Gavin appeared at the door with the table, and Jennifer clenched her jaw to avoid smiling. He had nailed on at least four new boards with several nails that were too big and were driven in crooked.

"It doesn't wobble anymore," he said.

"Let me have a look."

There was an odd expression on his face as he handed her the table, as if he knew it was a mess but hadn't quite admitted it to himself. Jennifer was not going to be the one to say it. To avoid discussing the look of the table, she put it on the floor and rocked it with her hand. It seemed a shade more stable.

"It's stronger now," she said.

"How do you think it looks."

"Fine."

"Is it okay?"

She reached out and hugged him.

"You're a good kid. It looks fine."

"I thought it was kind of a mess."

"Things always seem that way when you first do them. Put it in your room, and in a couple of days you'll be perfectly satisfied with it."

"Would my grandfather have thought it was okay?"

"He would have been very proud of you."

Gavin went off with the table, and Jennifer went to get herself another beer. She wanted to be drunk, felt hurt and joyful. Cindy would disapprove when she got the beer, and she was touched by the child's absurd concern. She could smell the hamburger frying and felt hungry.

"Smells good," she said.

"Don't help us," Cindy said.

"I just came for another beer."

"You're becoming an alcoholic."

"In my own small way."

"Besides, you'll get fat."

Alice looked up from the counter where she was cutting a green pepper.

"If I ever said that to my mother, she'd kill me."

"Shows you were properly brought up. Not to be cheeky."

She took her beer to the living-room. She thought about Gavin's repair of the table and wondered whether he was simply lacking in manual skills or whether he only needed the chance to develop them. It wasn't just the hands. She remembered her frustration at lacking the ability that her father and Harold both had to imagine things in three dimensions. Her father would draw a few lines on a piece of paper to work out in his head the construction of a piece of cabinet-work, and she would ask him to explain, but when he did she could never understand the explanation.

Up in the bedroom was the only piece of furniture she had that he'd made. It was a wedding present. He'd told her about it and showed it to her the night before she was married.

She was walking back from town with him. She couldn't remember how they'd come to be there together, though her father must have arranged it because he wanted to talk to her, and probably she had known. She always did. They had stopped at the bridge over the river.

It was a still June evening, and the light glinted on the fast movement of the water beneath the bridge. There was a clean cold smell, and near the edge where the current was slower, water-striders slid quickly over the surface. Farther down the river, they could see two boys fishing at the pool just before the river bent into the trees at Wilson's woods.

For a long time, they stood by the bridge in silence, their arms leaning on the edge. Jennifer's eyes took in, once again, the beauty of her father's hands. A bit of stain marked the fingers as it would for weeks once it had worked its way into the ridges of the skin. The nail on the index finger of his left hand had a strange curl to it from some past accident. The palms were wide, here and there ridged with calluses. The fingers were well shaped, but hard and knobbed from years of working with wood. The hands seemed almost to have become wood, hard and enduring, heavily grained from a slow growth to full maturity.

"You're sure then, that he's the one you want?"

The old Yorkshire accent was a little stronger, as always when he was feeling a strong emotion.

"I'd better be sure. I'm marrying him tomorrow."

The thought of Robert was out of place here. As she stood on the bridge over a river she had known all her life, beside her father, this fine sculpture carved by time out of the hard wood of his endurance, Robert, with all his quickness, all the flashes of light and dark, the terrible awareness, was a stranger. She couldn't understand the passion he had aroused in her.

"His people are well off."

"They seem to be."

They had gone through this before; her mother had asked questions about Robert's family after his first visit to the house one weekend in March, and her father had listened in silence to the answers.

"They must take us as we are."

Pride in it, and a strange sort of puzzlement. Her father, for all his political theories, the curious doctrines of Christian Socialism that came to him in pamphlets from Leeds that seemed more and more to belong 30 years in the past, was always a little puzzled by worldly success. He had no intuitive understanding of money and power, and he needed the pamphlets to provide a set of attitudes.

"I've made my own way, without asking for help from anyone."

Why did he need to say it, as if by marrying Robert she was judging him, being somehow critical of him for not being rich? It was a foolish fear and beneath him. She reached out and took his hand.

The water gurgled beneath their feet, the sun toward setting making the figures of the two boys luminous and vivid. There were a few wisps of cloud in the sky, and in the distance a hawk turned slowly.

"There's a chest in the workshop. It wants another coat of wax. Your mother has towels and bed-linen to fill it. I don't know if he'll like it."

He still couldn't bring himself to call Robert by name. He was polite, even tried to be friendly, but there was an uneasiness, a distrust.

She squeezed his hand.

"I was hoping you'd make us something."

Her father was looking down the river toward the boys. One of them had brought a fish ashore.

"That was Harold's favourite spot, down there," he said.

"You miss him a lot, don't you?"

"I'll miss you after tomorrow."

"But he was closest to you . . . I don't mind, I'm not jealous. I think Ross is."

"Ross is another sort altogether."

It was tolerant, and yet it wasn't. The man was never really easy with his younger son, but he and Harold had always been close until Harold had gone away to join the army. His death left a permanent wound.

"You've always made us proud and pleased. I hope the lad's worthy of you."

She reached out and hugged her father.

"You're just like every other father in the world when his daughter's getting married."

"And how should I be? Like a double-Dutch uncle?" He laughed, and they turned from the bridge and walked to the house. When they walked in, it was full of steam and the smell of fruit.

"Mother," Jennifer screamed, "what are you doing?"

"If I don't get this strawberry jam done tonight, the berries will go bad."

"But I'm getting married tomorrow."

"I'll be done in two shakes of a lamb's tail, then you can help me finish the cleaning."

"You could let the berries go bad for once. Tomorrow is my wedding day."

"The night before my wedding day, I finished making my dress, and on the day itself I worked a full eight-hour shift."

There was no use talking. Perhaps her mother had decided to make the jam because she couldn't bear to sit still. Or more likely because she resented the wedding, the fact that they were going for a trip in a car rented for them by Robert's father. Hot and sweaty in a cotton housedress, she looked like a farm woman.

"Would you like to see the chest?" her father said and moved her out the back door toward the workshop.

"Why did she have to do that?" Jennifer said as soon as they were outside the house.

"We've always had to be careful," her father said. "She can't bear to see good food wasted."

They walked across the yard to the small workshop. It was a familiar path to Jennifer. Often when she wanted company and reassurance she had come out to the workshop where her father (or in earlier days, her father and Harold) would be bent over the bench or the big work-table. In a corner the glue pot sat in a pot of hot water on a hotplate, the smell of the warm glue adding another organic layer to the clean smell of wood and sawdust and shavings. When she walked in, her father would stop the quiet humming that always went on as he worked for long enough to look up and smile at her. Then he would go back to work without speaking. She would find a quiet place in a corner to sit and watch.

Her father took out his keys, opened the workshop door

63

and reached inside to turn on the lights. Jennifer hadn't been inside the workshop much since she'd left home for university, and now walking out of the summer twilight into the familiar disorder made her feel as if her personality had separated into layers; she saw from a distance what had been close and familiar in the past. She was far from her father, yet far from Robert as well.

Her father led her through to the little room he'd built on the back as a finishing shop. There was a fan built into the wall to take away the fumes of the shellac and lacquer and paint, and in the corner a big air-compressor for the spray-gun. On a table in a corner was a piece of furniture covered by a sheet. Her father lifted the sheet away from it.

The dark red of the mahogany glowed. The design was simple, a rectangular lift-top chest standing on simple turned feet. He lifted the lid to show her the inside. He had lined it with cedar, and as Jennifer leaned over the chest to look in, the clean sharp smell of the unfinished cedar was strong.

"It's beautiful," she said.

She sat on an old stool in the corner of the finishing shop while her father put on a final coat of wax, time lapping back on itself like an eddy. Then they returned to the house, and Jennifer worked to exhaustion helping her mother clean the house. She went to bed and woke to the confusing pell-mell rush of her wedding day.

Robert's parents arrived early. His mother seemed heavier than Jennifer had remembered, and to move more stiffly, her shoulders held oddly because of some rheumatic pain. His father was stiff and righteous, his grey eyes cold and distant and his manner formal and disapproving. Her own father made one or two gestures of friendship, and when these were ignored, withdrew into his own proud anger. Robert was painfully aware of the awkwardness of it all, his face almost transparent, as if the bones and nerves would soon appear on the surface. Jennifer wanted to hold him and make him safe from it all. At the small reception in the church hall, Robert's mother lit a cigarette, and one of the women waiting on the tables asked her to put it out.

It was at the reception that Jennifer realized that Robert's older sister hadn't come. Robert explained that she couldn't bring her Jewish husband to meet her father and wouldn't come without him.

At last, at the end of a confused and jangled day, she hugged her mother and father, Robert shook her father's hand, and they drove away. She moved close to Robert, and as the car moved down the grey highway, he put his hand between her thighs, and she pressed her legs together, gripping it tight there.

Jennifer drank the last of her beer. If the food wasn't ready soon, she was going to have another. She felt in that gay and sensitive mood in which she would have liked to drink all evening. Go to court with a hangover.

Poor Eugene. He'd come to her asking for love, and she, who'd grown up surrounded by love, had refused him.

"Dinner's ready."

It was Cindy's voice from the kitchen. Jennifer made her way to the table, stopping to shout up the stairs and make sure that Gavin was coming. The two girls had made a bouquet of autumn leaves and dead grass and set it in the middle of the table. They had set out red place-mats and white plates.

"How marvellous you are," Jennifer said. Alice smiled, but Cindy refused to acknowledge that she might be pleased by the praise.

The spaghetti sauce was a little greasy, and Jennifer wondered whether they had poured the fat off the hamburger when they fried it. She kept her mouth shut about it.

Cindy and Gavin had a couple of minor spats over dinner, and afterward the two girls departed to Alice's house.

"You got homework?" Jennifer asked Gavin.

"A whole bunch."

Jennifer did the dishes and then took out some new material on the symbols that she had just got from Toronto. She spent the evening with it, stopping only to see that the children got to bed.

When she got up in the morning, she found she was very nervous about testifying. She wanted someone to reassure her, to tell her what to wear, but there was only the silence of the empty house. Who was she to be in court? What role was she to play? She must improvise a face appropriate to the legal proceedings. She searched through her closet and found a dark green dress that she'd worn when she was teaching. It was conventional. It would have to do. Court didn't start till ten o'clock, so for an hour she sat reading. Rosamund was destroying Lydgate. As, in Robert's eyes, she had destroyed him; he had wanted something from her, she had never known what it was, but he knew it as what would make him a different and better man.

She put down the book and set out for the building where the hearing would be held. It was a plain brick building situated in the shadow of the grand nineteenth-century stone courthouse with its noble dome and pillars and fountain and curving drive. Because she knew she was early, Jennifer walked a roundabout route, going down through the university and past the hospital to the lake.

As she passed the hospital, she reminded herself that she must phone Barbara again. She had only spoken to her once since she had been released. It was easy to forget the needs of your friends once the dramatic moment was past.

Her children wouldn't have their class today, but probably only Melinda would notice. What was to be done with Melinda since her mother rejected her? Would she spend her whole life guiding an electronic wheelchair down the bare corridors of that hospital, eating an acceptable diet prepared and served without love, now and then taken out in good weather by one of the orderlies? Someone should take her into a proper home.

The lake was in front of her. It was a grey breezy day, and the water was choppy. Jennifer checked her watch, not wanting to be early, but eager for the court appearance to be over. To put on the mask of citizen, then quickly take it off and retire into a careful privacy. Robert, objecting to the linguistic barbarity of the recent use of Ms. for Miss or Mrs., liked to suggest that the sexual distinction be dropped as well, and on the model of the French Revolution, everyone be called Citizen. He could get no-one to take him seriously.

Arrived at the court, Jennifer found a small crowd gathered in the hall outside the two courtrooms. Everything was shapeless and disorganized. No majesty of the law here. Most of those gathered were young and poor. Now and then a lawyer appeared, sleek in a three-piece suit and expensive haircut, coming out a doorway from the secret places at the back of the building, consulting in a corner with a client in dirty jeans with cuts on his face and hands, then disappearing again. It would be easy, she thought, to see the legal apparatus as no more than an expensive way of imposing discipline on the indigent and rebellious.

A couple of young policemen in neatly pressed uniforms moved in and out of the courtroom without much to do, apparently, but be present in a symbolic capacity. The detective who had interviewed Jennifer appeared. He was a dark man with straight grey hair. He shook her hand.

"Hello, Mrs. Mallen. We're in Courtroom 1. You can sit down and wait in there if you'd like. Once the hearing starts all the witnesses will be excluded."

"How long will it be until I testify?"

"Hard to say. It depends how long the defence spends cross-examining the earlier witnesses. Probably late this morning or after lunch."

He turned toward the door of the building, where a girl in her twenties had entered with a woman who appeared to be her mother. The detective walked away from Jennifer and moved toward the two women. The girl was stocky, with pale skin and mousy hair, but when she greeted the detective she smiled, and her face became almost pretty. This was the girl Eugene had raped. It all seemed so unlikely, here in this undramatic setting, more like a high-school principal's office after school, the girl appearing with her mother to confront some minor problem.

Jennifer studied the girl's face, wondering just how she had been affected, how deeply she might have been hurt. Like any woman, Jennifer had thought about rape occasionally, tried to imagine her own response, but her imagination failed her. She couldn't know how it would be.

She walked into the courtroom. It was new, clean, meaningless. At the front a slightly raised bench for the judge. Lawyers' tables. A few benches for spectators. The only part of the court that caught the eye was the glass-walled box for the accused. As Jennifer was about to sit on one of the benches, Eugene was led in through the door behind the judge's bench. He was wearing a suit and tie. He looked thinner and very young. His hair was combed forward so that the scar was almost invisible. He looked vulnerable and innocent except perhaps for the slight twist to his badly shaped lips. He was young. So young and miserable.

Could all this have been avoided? What would have happened if she had let him stay at her house while she had gone to visit Barbara?

As he walked toward the box, a uniformed OPP officer at his side, a lawyer in a black legal gown stood up from the table and came to him. He took Eugene by the arm and whispered quietly. Eugene seemed hardly to listen. His eyes moved around the small courtroom. He saw Jennifer sitting on the back bench and raised his hand to her in a kind of ironic salute.

The lawyer finished, and Eugene was led toward the box. He stopped at the rail, looking toward Jennifer and smiling. She went to meet him.

"You came to see me put on exhibition," he said. "I always knew I'd end up in a freak show."

"I'm a witness for the prosecution."

"Why?"

"They can force me to testify."

"I knew you wouldn't do it unless they made you."

"Are you still in jail?"

He nodded.

"They won't grant me bail because I'm a crazy."

The police officer moved toward them.

"Better go in and sit down. They'll be ready to go soon."

Eugene went into the box, and Jennifer returned to her seat on the bench. Why was she here? It wasn't true to suggest, as Eugene had, that they had made her come. It was misleading for her to say she could be forced to testify. She could, but she was there to offer her bit of information. To bear witness. But did she believe in the law? Eugene was sick. Why put him in prison?

He could perhaps be cured, be taught to be human in the ways he had missed. It was such a waste of his sensitivity and intelligence to put him away, to fasten his future to the mistakes of his past. Yet a courtroom of men and women who assumed that they themselves were free and capable of development would judge Eugene on the basis of a single action, as if that summed up his being.

The victim and her mother appeared at the door of the courtroom. The girl looked toward Eugene. He was talking to his lawyer again, over the wall of the box, and she could only see the back of his head. She whispered to her mother, and the older woman looked toward him. The look was murderous, and for a moment, Jennifer felt herself in the woman's place, looking at the figure of the man who had violated her daughter. Hurt him, give him pain, violate him, send him to prison where hard men will bugger him to death, she heard herself saying.

Which side could she be on? The side of the court, per-

69

haps, the side of legal propriety, a game played by the rules. Or was that a mere evasion? The bureaucrat's escape: flee the anxiety of painful and irreconcilable conflict in an absolute loyalty to procedure. Eichmann the filing clerk.

A few more people came in and sat down, the lawyers took their places. The clerk came in, checked the room and disappeared to get the judge. "Order," he called as he came back, and everyone rose for the judge's entrance.

It was Tom Van Every. Jennifer thought she saw his eyes catch a glimpse of her, but his face remained impassive as the lawyers bowed, and he took his seat. Jennifer remembered her last meeting with Van Every, embarrassed by her own self-righteousness. How could she give evidence in front of him? He was listening to the reading of the indictment. He was the court, the human embodiment of justice, bibbed and gowned, no longer like ordinary men. Had he left all his weaknesses behind?

The defence lawyer was making motions for a ban on the publication of evidence and the exclusion of witnesses. Van Every asked all the witnesses to leave the court. Jennifer rose along with the rape victim, the police detective and a couple of others she didn't know. One looked like a doctor.

The young girl went and sat on a wodden bench in an alcove. Jennifer went past her and outside the main door. As she stood there, the wind from the lake blowing her hair, two people, a young man with a thin beard and greasy hair and a fat girl, came out the door and pushed past her.

"That lawyer's a fucken dummy."

"I think you're lucky to get off with a fine."

"Where am I going to get the money? I shouldn't ever have been convicted."

They went off down the path to the street, the man walking swiftly, the girl hurrying to stay with him. Their voices faded. When they reached the street, he stopped for a second to let a car pass, and the girl got close enough to take his arm. She clung tightly to him, and he allowed it but wouldn't look at her.

Jennifer went back inside, took her place on the bench in the alcove. She and the girl smiled but didn't speak.

For the next two hours, she sat on the bench, mentally composing essays on the social and psychological effects of boredom. Now and then a witness would come out of the courtroom or another would go in. In the other courtroom on the opposite side of the entrance hall, groups of people went in and out much more quickly. She asked one of the policemen why, and he said that most were there for remands or sentencing or were pleading guilty. Their confrontation with the law was brief.

At last it was her turn. She was taken into the courtroom to the small witness-box in the corner near the judge. Tom Van Every's eyes met hers, but there was no response.

She took her oath, and the crown attorney moved toward her. He was a large slow man with heavy glasses, with something swaying and bear-like about his movements.

"Would you tell me your name please."

"Jennifer Mallen."

"And where do you live?"

"395 Earl Street."

"That's in the city of Kingston."

"Yes."

"What is your marital status?"

"I'm divorced."

"And were you at home on the evening of September 24th?"

"Yes."

"Who was there with you?"

"My two children."

"What are their ages?"

"Eleven and thirteen."

"Do you know the defendant, Eugene Slyfield?"

"Yes."

"Could you tell me how you met him?"

"I work at the Ontario Hospital teaching a group of handicapped children. I met him there."

"Did the defendant come to your house on the evening of September 24th?"

"Yes he did."

"Had you invited him?"

"Not formally. When we met at the hospital, he said he'd like to come and visit sometime. I said perhaps that would be possible."

"Were you surprised to see him at your house?"

"Yes I was."

"Do you know what time he arrived?"

"It was about 7.35."

"And do you know what time he left?"

"About ten minutes later."

"Is there any particular reason you noticed these times?"

"Yes, I was on my way to visit a friend in the hospital, and since visiting hours end at eight, I was worried about getting there in time to see her."

"Can you tell me what kind of emotional state the defendant was in?"

The defence lawyer rose to object that Jennifer wasn't an expert witness, there was a little byplay between judge and lawyers, and the crown attorney rephrased the question.

"Did Eugene seem calm?"

"No. He was quite excited. Especially when I explained that I had to go to the hospital and that he'd have to leave."

"He didn't want to leave?"

"No."

"But he finally did."

"Yes."

She hadn't told the detective about the struggle with the phone or at the door. It hadn't occurred to him to ask about a struggle, and she hadn't brought it up.

"To sum up, just after 7.45 the defendant, in a somewhat excited state, left your house on Earl Street."

He was carefully placing Eugene in the neighbourhood of the rape at the appropriate time. Jennifer could see Eugene's eyes on her. Until now he'd been looking in another direction, but now their eyes met. She was about to solder a link in the chain of evidence. She looked away.

"Yes," she said.

She felt like Judas. The crown attorney returned to his table, and the defence attorney rose. His name was unfamiliar, and she suspected that Eugene's family had hired him in Ottawa. He was small with a neat muscular body. His lips were tight as he approached her.

"Mrs. Mallen, you've told my friend that you met Eugene at the hospital."

"Yes."

"How did that happen?"

"I think we met in the hall."

"Can you remember the circumstances?"

"I believe he said hello to me in the hall, and I answered him."

"He was friendly."

"Yes."

"And you accepted his overture of friendship."

"I spoke to him."

She could see where the question was going, to suggest that she had led Eugene on, but she wouldn't back off and be apologetic.

"Had you often met at the hospital?"

"Three or four times, I think."

"And it was always friendly."

"Yes."

"Who brought up the idea that Eugene might visit your house?"

"He did."

"Do you remember how it happened?"

"I think he said that maybe he'd come to my house sometime, and I said maybe so."

"You agreed."

"I said maybe he could come. At some undefined time."

"But you didn't say No, he couldn't come."

"No."

"So you had a friendly relationship at the hospital, and when he asked if he could come to your home you agreed."

"I agreed that it was a possibility."

"What is your work at the hospital?"

"I teach children with intellectual and motor handicaps. It's an experimental program using a new symbolic language that's used at the Centre for Crippled Children."

"What are your professional qualifications?"

"I've been a teacher here and in England."

"Do you have any professional qualifications in psychology?"

"No."

"So you're not in a position to make expert judgments about emotional disturbances."

"That's correct. I'm a teacher."

His insinuating manner was getting under her skin. She wondered if Tom Van Every enjoyed seeing her discomfiture. He must, after the way she'd treated him.

"Why did you allow yourself to get involved with Eugene if you lacked the professional qualifications?"

"I didn't feel I was 'getting involved' as you put it. I tried to be polite and friendly."

How flat and ridiculous that sounded. Like a schoolgirl, president of the Junior Red Cross, being nice to the class oddball.

"But you did allow him to feel that he could come to your house?"

"I suppose so."

He had made his point. Everyone in the courtroom was watching her.

"Let's turn to the night in question, the evening of September 24th. Eugene came to visit you that night?"

74

"Yes."

"Did you invite him in?"

"I suppose so."

"You were being polite and friendly."

"I couldn't just shut the door in his face."

"What happened after you invited him into the house?"

"I explained that it wasn't a good time for a visit."

"Why was that."

"I explained that before. I was about to visit a friend in the hospital, and visiting hours were nearly over."

"Was Eugene upset when you tried to send him away?"

"Yes."

"Couldn't you have phoned the hospital and postponed the visit till the next day?"

"No."

"Why not? Here was a boy with emotional problems who felt that he was invited to your home, and when he arrives, he's immediately sent away."

"I couldn't postpone the visit."

"Why was that?"

Jennifer paused. Her eyes moved quickly around the court. The faces were still, watching her. The moment went on. The only face not watching her was Tom Van Every. He was making a note on the pad in front of him, avoiding her eyes.

"It has nothing to do with this hearing," she said, "but I had good reasons."

"I'd like to know what they were."

There was a voice from beside her.

"I don't see the relevance of this."

It was Tom Van Every. The defence attorney looked toward him.

"It's all part of the picture of what we know about the defendant that evening."

"You can deal with the consequences. I don't think you need Mrs. Mallen's private life. She's not on trial here."

The defence attorney turned back toward her.

"What happened when you told Eugene he'd have to leave?"

"He was upset. He didn't want to go."

"Were you worried about what he might do after he left your house?"

"I don't know. Mainly I wanted him to leave."

"You didn't care what happened as long as you got rid of him?"

Jennifer held herself still and breathed slowly. She was to be held responsible that Eugene had raped the girl. Was that fair? Was she responsible for Eugene?

"I had to leave the house. There were two children there with me. I wanted to get rid of him."

"No matter what the consequences."

"If you say so."

"I want to know what you say."

"I hardly knew him. I was concerned about my friend and about my children."

"Would you say you were more concerned not to be late for an appointment than to help Eugene."

"I couldn't help Eugene."

"Didn't he feel you could help him?"

"He was wrong."

Jennifer felt stolid now, wooden and stiff and beleagred. She would go on. Whatever she said today, she would have to say again at the trial. She was tired of it, no longer cared if she said something foolish.

"Did you finally persuade Eugene to leave?"

"Yes."

"How did you do that?"

Jennifer hesitated for a second, saw Eugene's face. She must try to protect him.

"I don't exactly remember."

"Is it true that you pushed him out the door of your house?"

76

Eugene had told him that, had betrayed her, tried to use her.

"Only after he'd knocked me down."

The crown attorney and the detective looked up from the table and stared toward her. Eugene was behind them, a still pale figure enclosed in the box. Jennifer felt sorry now that the words were out, wanted to take them back and apologize to him. It wasn't his fault.

The defence attorney had noticed the look she was getting from the prosecution table.

"Did you tell the police that he knocked you down?"

She knew what was coming now. She had to admit this defence lawyer was very quick.

"No I didn't."

"Why was that?"

"I didn't want to make it any worse for Eugene than I had to. I guess I felt somehow guilty or responsible."

Was that the truth? At least it was what he wanted. He would leave her alone now. She watched as the tight strong-looking body turned away from her. She was frustrated by the sense that she hadn't made him understand, that he had not felt the fear and jangling chaos of that night. Maybe it was true that there were no innocent bystanders, but that was too simple. The difference between that night and her testimony was the difference between a painting and its interpretation. The court was only a game of lies and half-truths given ritual form.

The defence attorney thanked her and sat down. The crown began to rise as if to ask further questions, but thought better of it.

From beside her, she heard the voice of the judge thanking her as she stepped from the witness-box and began to walk from the court. She tried to avoid catching anyone's eye. She wanted to be invisible, walked quickly out of the courtroom and through the lobby to the door. Behind her she heard Van Every call a recess for lunch.

She left the building and walked blindly down the street toward her house. She breathed deeply, thankful for the cool windy air that seemed like an offer of health and strength. Her hands were shaking. She couldn't stop them.

She had walked a couple of blocks when she saw a car stop half a block in front of her. A familiar figure got out and walked toward her. Tom Van Every.

"You had a rough time," he said. "Can I buy you lunch?"

"No, thanks."

She wanted to run, and yet she didn't want to be alone.

"Are you sure?"

"No, I'm not sure. I don't know what I want."

"Come and get in the car."

It was a Datsun, not what she imagined a judge driving.

"What you need is a drink and a good meal."

He drove to a restaurant downtown. There was only one table left, against the wall. As they walked toward it, Jennifer felt exposed. She carried with her the unease of the courtroom, but once they were seated at the table, she felt a little better. The waitress came toward them.

"I know that girl," he said, surprised.

He smiled at her as she moved between the tables, and her face registered recognition. She was a slim girl with dark blond curly hair and fine features.

"I thought your father said you were in England, Cassie."

"I came back a couple of weeks ago. I was running out of money, and I think my aunt had had enough of me."

"Are you going to university in the fall?"

"I don't know. In the summer I'm going to work at the riding-stables."

Jennifer looked across the table. The man's smiling face seemed so much at ease here. She felt an outsider. The girl took their orders for drinks and left.

"Her father used to be my partner. I never quite realized how grown up she was."

Jennifer nodded. She seemed to have nothing to say. She

didn't understand why he had come looking for her.

"Were you prepared for the kind of treatment you got in court?"

"I was nervous, but not for any good reason. I'd never been in court before."

"The adversary system has a lot to be said for it, but now and then it leads to some excessive aggressiveness."

"Will it really do any good to suggest that I was somehow responsible?"

"It may. It's a classic defence manoeuvre. Spread the blame as far as you can, bring up any mitigating circumstance, anything that might sway any member of the jury toward voting not guilty."

"I have been feeling bad about that night."

"What else could you have done? Surely Barbara had the first claim on your concern."

'That's what I thought."

"How is she?"

"Seems much as usual. As if it was all a temporary aberration. But then most of the time she doesn't let on much."

"I don't like to think about her. It's hard to know how to deal with something you did that you know was wrong or foolish. There's a nasty feeling every time the memory comes back. Worse because there's nothing to be done about it."

Jennifer felt herself stiffening with resistance to what he was saying. She must maintain her loyalty to Barbara. Not let him explain it away or make her feel for him. She was on the other side.

"You still hold it against me, don't you?"

"Yes."

"Is there any way I can make you feel differently about it?"

"I don't think so."

The girl brought their drinks. Jennifer had ordered a martini.

79

"Should we have been discussing something that has to do with the trial?" Jennifer said, wanting to get the subject away from Barbara.

"Strictly speaking, no, but most of my decisions at the preliminary will be procedural ones. There's no real doubt that the case will be sent to trial. I was surprised to see you as one of the witnesses, and if this were the trial I'd disqualify myself, but my connection with your testimony is pretty slight."

The careful weighing of words gave his speech a sense of sureness. Jennifer was afraid that she had begun almost to like the man.

"Barbara told me you'd lived in England for several years."

"Nearly ten."

"In London?"

"Yes."

"You must miss it."

"Sometimes. Though not the obvious things. Strange things like the neighbourhood newsagent. Unimportant and not especially attractive places where we went walking. Things like that."

"True nostalgia is a longing for things you didn't even like."

"Yes," she said. She couldn't help smiling. It was true. The mere thought that things were far off in space and time made them desirable.

The girl came back to take their order. Jennifer noticed that Van Every responded quickly to women, even this girl. Nothing that could be called flirtation, but it was clear that he noticed that she was attractive, that he couldn't help it. Jennifer felt a little jealous of the girl's youth and heedlessness. Her uniform was worn sloppily, but it made no difference to how attractive she looked.

As Jennifer sat quietly by, there was some mysterious music going on between the two of them, the man discovering that the girl was now sexually mature, the girl suddenly seeing this friend of the family as an attractive male. All of it unspoken, likely always to remain unspoken. It seemed abstract, impersonal, like a concept one might study in physics. Men were like that and women were like this, and both were driven toward conjunction. The old dance. Jennifer was the neutral observer. Was this to be her life now? To observe, understand, be of assistance. It seemed to be the direction in which she was moving professionally; perhaps it was her personal destiny as well.

The girl finished writing the order and left their table.

"Can I ask you some more questions about yourself?" he said, turning back to her.

"That's an odd thing to say."

"Well, since I'm established in your mind as someone you dislike or disapprove of, I thought it might be importunate."

"Go right ahead."

Jennifer smiled to herself at his strangely blunt manner. What at first seemed almost pompous was just a manner of speech. His courtroom manner. He asked her about her work and the children and how long she'd been divorced, stopping only when the food was on the table.

"I hope you didn't think I was cross-examining you? It always seems to me that if you want to know things, you should ask."

"It's the only way."

She was still smiling to herself as she ate her lunch. Against her will, she was having a good time. She enjoyed telling him things about herself, watching his bright brown eyes focus on her face as she spoke. She understood how Barbara had fallen for him. As they finished eating, he checked his watch to see how soon he was due back in court.

"I'll drive you home on my way back," he said.

"Are you sure you have time?"

"Yes."

Jennifer was staring around the room at the men and women from downtown businesses who came here for lunch. It was a long time since she'd gone out anyplace. She was becoming a bit of a hermit. She didn't much want to go back to the hospital this afternoon. The thought of the small room and the struggling minds and bodies of her four children was a bit oppressive. How long would she go on locked into that room and those lives?

"Are you going to work this afternoon?" he said.

"I was just battling the temptation not to."

"It must be very demanding work."

"Yes."

The waitress brought their coffee. She wasn't wearing a brassière and Jennifer could see the shape of her young breasts under the waitress' uniform. She moved well, and Jennifer remembered her comment about working with horses. Soon Cindy would be this age, though Cindy was different, more elegant, less animal. One almost expected this girl to have an acrid animal scent about her.

When the bill came, Jennifer insisted on paying her share, though he tried to stop her. It seemed a matter of loyalty to Barbara. Was it absurd to see it that way? Still, she paid.

He drove her home, and as they stopped outside, he looked toward her.

"Can I see you again?" he said.

"Would that be wise?"

"Probably not."

4

The ringing of the phone tore into her sleep, brought her up, panicky, out of unconsciousness. Trapped, something was holding her down. The phone rang again. It was Tom's arm, she pulled away, climbed from the bed, her hands reaching wildly through the dark. She found the receiver and got it to her ear.

"Jenny, it's Ross."

"What's the matter?"

"It's Mum. She's dying."

"What happened?"

"She's been sick for quite a while, but she didn't tell anyone. I tried to get her to go to the doctor, but she wouldn't. She just sat out there. I didn't realize how bad she was. She finally phoned me tonight, and by the time I got there, she could hardly move."

She could hear the strain as he controlled his voice.

"Is she in the hospital?"

"Yes, but they can't really do anything. The liver's completely shot. They told me to phone you."

"How long?"

"Maybe only a few hours."

"What time is it?"

"Nearly two."

"I'll get there as soon as I can."

She hung up the phone, sat down on the bed. The window was outlined by light from the street, and her eyes were beginning to adjust to the dark. She could make out the shapes of the furniture. She heard Tom's voice from behind her.

"What is it?"

"My mother. She's dying. I've got to go. I'm trying to think what's the fastest way."

"Take my car."

"I can't do that."

"It's the quickest."

"But your wife . . ."

"I'll just tell her it broke down. I'll go home in a cab and rent a car tomorrow. It happened once before when the car was in the garage for a couple of days. Eleanor doesn't drive. She never pays any attention to the car."

He moved across the bed and put his hand on her shoulder.

"Take it."

"Are you sure?"

"Yes."

"I guess it's the best chance of getting there while she's still alive."

She reached out and turned on the light, shut her eyes for a second against the brightness. When she opened them, she saw herself naked with a kind of shock. The large heavy breasts hung toward her belly where the pubic hair was still damp and matted from making love to Tom. She turned toward him. He was climbing from the other side of the bed. His body was wide, strong, dark.

Jennifer got up and began to dress herself. Across the room, Tom was putting on his clothes.

"Do you really want me to take your car?"

"Yes."

Jennifer found a few extra clothes and put them in a handbag. She counted the money out of the box in her bedside table, then brushed out her hair and put it in a neat bun. Tom stood watching her. She looked around the room, took a moment to pull up the covers on the bed, then walked quietly downstairs.

Tom called a cab while Jennifer found a pen and a piece of paper and printed a note to Gavin and Cindy, telling them to phone Mrs. Buttle, a neighbour who had looked after them before, and also to phone Robert. In the morning she could call back and see that everything was all right.

Tom's cab arrived almost immediately. She didn't want him to go. If only he could make the trip with her. He gave her the car keys, kissed her, then vanished into the darkness. The house was silent. In a couple more minutes, she was ready to go. She left the hall light on, but locked the door behind her.

It was strange to be sitting behind the wheel of Tom's car, but everything in the last few weeks had been like that, sudden and unpredictable. When Tom had come to her house to talk about Barbara, Jennifer had insulted him. Now he was her lover. She hated to think about Barbara now.

Her life had been simple before, lonely, dogged by pain, but simple and direct. Now she was compromised. Everything was such a mockery, Jennifer pushing Eugene out of the house because Barbara had attempted suicide and then having an affair with the man who had brought her friend to that attempt. Looked at like that, from outside, as the lawyer had looked at her behaviour in cross-examining her, it was grotesque, and yet as it happened, it all made sense.

And Tom? It was terrifying that he no longer seemed to care if his wife found out. He was prepared to leave her, but Jennifer didn't let him talk about it. She couldn't let herself think of his daughter growing up without him, couldn't accept the responsibility of destroying a marriage, though she had to admit the truth, that she wanted him, that she was postponing the disaster out of some kind of superstition or fear.

Barbara had phoned a couple of days before, and they had arranged to go to a concert together. What would happen when Barbara found out? Would she try to kill herself again? Jennifer hadn't the strength to consider such a possibility. She had always thought of herself as a strong person, but she was spread too thin. Maybe that was just a consequence of age, more demands made on the personality as the sources of energy became slower and fewer.

The road unrolled ahead of her to the home of her childhood, her mother dying in a hospital bed.

Why had they never been close? Her mother, in some subdued and undefined way, had preferred the boys, especially Ross, her youngest, and she had almost resented Jennifer's success in school, her chance to get an education and travel. She was herself a smalltown girl whose only adventure had been to leave home for a clerical job in Hamilton, where she had met the young English cabinetmaker she was to marry, returning to live near her home town when the land for a house was offered to them by an uncle who was giving up his farm and wanted to make things easier for a favourite niece. The year they started building the house, things had seemed, if not easy, at least hopeful. Then the depression had struck, the factory where her father worked went bankrupt, and they began the long years of struggling, not having the money to finish work on the house so that, until Jennifer was in her teens, it resembled a tarpaper shack.

Jennifer had been born into the middle of the worst period of her parents' life, and she sometimes wondered if her mother had always resented her a little because of that, attached to her all the anxiety of that period. Her father had gone anyplace he could get a day's work. Her mother had gone out as a cleaning woman, and that was a humiliation neither of her parents ever forgot. In a way, the pregnancy that ended that must have been a relief to them, however terrifying the loss of money. Certainly her father had spoken of it that way.

Jennifer was too young to remember the worst years. By the time her memories began, in the late thirties, their life was a constant struggle with debt, a small doctor's bill when Jennifer had pneumonia enough to begin a fierce argument because neither of her parents saw any way it could be paid, but the very worst was over, partly because they knew they had survived the worst and could continue, and partly because Harold, her older brother, was a serious and well grown boy who did odd jobs and brought in a bit of money. When he was fourteen, he left school and got a full-time job. Early in the war, the furniture factory reopened with government contracts for wooden parts used in the De Havilland Mosquito.

Until Harold went overseas, he and his father worked side by side in the factory, leaving together in the morning and arriving home together at night. Nights and weekends, they worked together in the small workshop behind the house which they had built of scrap lumber. They seemed more like brothers than father and son, and Jennifer, though she was welcome in the workshop and liked to go there and watch them, was expected to spend most of her time with her mother, but the woman and the girl didn't have any special closeness or understanding. When Jennifer was seven years old, Ross was born. He was always to be her mother's favourite, and Jennifer lapsed into the no-man's-land of middle children. Her mother was often impatient with her, and Jennifer lived in a dreamy resentful silence. Harold was her hero, but he was too busy to have a lot of time for her. She had never doubted her father's fondness for her, but she had no place in his life until gradually, with her success in school, she won a place, as the child who made him proud, who got the family name in the local newspaper by her minor academic achievements. She began to feel that she was to be his revenge on the world for the hardness of his life. While he read avidly the strange pamphlets of the Christian Socialist League that came to him from England in their thin brown wrappers, his emotional belief was not in the organizing abilities of the workers, but in the cleverness of his own daughter. It was that which would put things right.

Jennifer pulled off the road at a service-centre and got herself a cup of coffee. Not that she felt sleepy. She was surprised at how wide awake she was, for she had only dozed off for a few minutes after making love. She thought of Tom arriving home, then stopped herself. She wouldn't know about that.

The black surface of the highway carried her through the night. She drove as fast as she dared, determined to reach her mother while the woman was still alive. She had failed in love toward her mother in a hundred small ways. She had never really touched her life.

Her mind went back to Tom, she couldn't help it. When they were together, it seemed simple. He was very straightforward, the kind of man, she supposed, that she was always attracted to now, because they were different from Robert. She loved Tom as she had loved Colin. And Robert? Who was to say? She had married him, they had conceived children together. It was something different.

Tom often brought back the memory of England and Colin. They shared that directness, the immensely relaxing simplicity. She had met Colin on one of the Aldermaston marches when she and Robert were active in the CND. He worked for a wholesale vegetable supplier, and Robert would always refer to him as "Jennifer's pious greengrocer."

When Robert left her for the first time, Colin had become her lover. What a lovely soft slow man he had been. They had a standing joke about the things he meant to read. That included almost everything.

"I meant to read it on the tube going in to work," he would say with a beautiful puzzled smile over why he hadn't done it. After watching Robert race argumentatively through the *Guardian*, the *Times*, the *New Statesman*, *Tribune*, it was so winning to see Colin begin an article, his forehead becoming more and more wrinkled as the problems of that particular situation spread in his mind and he tried to work them out. Often he'd stop halfway through and sit rubbing his nose, overwhelmed by complexity.

And yet in some indirect and roundabout way, he always knew what his response should be. He was one of the first CND people to be sent to jail.

Oh Colin, you sweet man, you pious greengrocer, how I love you even now.

Of the times that she and Robert were separated and came back together, that was the one when she was closest to saying No, that she didn't want to go back with him, and though she did go back, for a year afterward, until Cindy was born, she had walked through her life like a ghost playing her part. Probably it was a mistake for her to have returned to Robert then, to prolong their agony and involve children in it.

But Colin had never asked her to stay. Not that he sent her away, but he never said the words, and that made her suspect that Colin, with his great insight, believed she ought to return to Robert. And Robert, after a disastrous affair with an ambitious young literary agent had ended up in a therapeutic community run by a woman psychiatrist and was convinced that he had won his way to a new understanding and clarity. That he was a new man.

When he returned, he was changed, there could be no doubting it. He wanted children, something he had fled from previously, and Cindy was conceived within a couple of months. It was a strange period. Robert, in his new self, was oddly flat and humourless, no irony, no edge of bitterness. He had shut off parts of himself and left a blank. Over his work-table was a quotation from Freud: "we are never so defenceless against suffering as when we love." Jennifer didn't find it reassuring, though she couldn't deny its truthfulness, for through it all she was longing for Colin, calling him on the phone now and then, weeping inside through the conversations. All past now. It was all over and done.

How were she and Tom to go on? She had achieved, she had thought, at least a little clarity, but now it was all befogged, muddied. She was blundering, blind among the blind. Could she say that she wanted Tom, that she would have him whatever the cost? Not yet. But how she did want him.

There were a few cars on the highway, more than she would have expected at this hour, but there were still long spells of empty road. On this kind of highway, the more attention you paid to your driving, the harder and more boring it was. It was better to let your mind wander and take in automatically the few facts that were necessary to direct the car.

She thought of the headlines in the newspaper she'd read at suppertime, the threats of an Arab oil boycott, the Albertans who were saying that they should let the easterners freeze in the dark. In the face of such threats, she was helpless to defend herself or her children.

Jennifer drove on. Now and then she'd check her watch, and at one of the service-centres she pulled off the road, used the toilet and got another cup of coffee from a tired looking woman with dyed blond hair and lipstick that didn't match. In the morning she'd have to phone Irving at the hospital.

She hadn't got any further with Jeffrey. How many months or years would it take to reach him? Could McAdam be right that the cost was just too high? No.

At Toronto, she left Highway 401 and turned north. She was beginning to tire, her back and legs stiff from sitting in one position. In the east the colour of the sky was changing, and the shapes of the bare trees and empty fields began to appear beside the road. It was a cloudy day, and there was no sunrise, only a gradual expansion of grey light over the November landscape.

When she reached town, she decided, she'd drive directly to the hospital. There was no point going to Ross's house. If her mother was still alive, Ross would be at the hospital with her. As the car moved over the last few miles of road, fatigue spread through Jennifer's body like dye spreading through water. It was morning now, and here and there she'd see someone at the door of a house or walking to a nearby car to drive to work. Signs of warm life in the pale bleached countryside. Familiar landmarks appeared, the fallen barn on the McNaughton place, the curve of road by a high rock face, interspersed with unfamiliar houses, a Keutucky Fried Chicken outlet she'd never seen before, a new arena.

To reach the hospital, she turned at the second traffic-light and drove along an empty, familiar, tree-lined street. Grafnell Street. To walk from her home on the edge of town to the high school, she'd walked three blocks along Grafnell Street, five days a week for five years.

There was a new porch on the Greggs' house. That must mean that the Gregg brothers were dead. The town was different. She was a stranger here where she had spent her first eighteen years. She drove past the high school, the scene of her small triumphs, the only place she'd ever stood out from the crowd, taking eleven papers in Grade XIII instead of the nine required for university admission, winning most of the scholarships, then discovering with a shock when she reached university that almost everyone in her class had that kind of high school record, and that while she was a good student, she would never again be thought a brilliant one. In her first year she went out a couple of times with a math student from Hespeler who'd gone through the same shock. He could talk of nothing else, and after Christmas he left the university and returned home.

Jennifer parked the car on the street in front of the red-brick hospital building. When the engine stopped, she sat still for a moment, closed her eyes and tried to let the sound of the car drain out of her.

The small reception area of the hospital was empty. She walked down the hall, unsure where she might find Ross or her mother. She noticed a nursing-station, but the nurse on duty wasn't there. Jennifer stood for a moment and waited, but when no-one appeared, she walked on. The patients in the rooms she passed were mostly asleep under the heavy white hospital sheets. Here and there bandages were visible or a limb in traction. A young girl lay uncovered, her pale legs showing beneath the hospital gown. Beyond the window of her room, the light was grey over the flat asphalt of the parking-lot.

A white figure appeared at the end of the hall. Jennifer made her way toward her.

"I'm looking for my mother. Mrs. Hopcroft. My brother phoned, and I've driven all night."

The sound of her own voice was odd in the high empty hall. Jennifer waited for the woman to announce that her mother was dead.

"Is she in Intensive Care?"

"I don't know."

The woman walked to the nursing-station. She was heavy-set, and the dress was tight over her hips. She had a short quiet conversation on the phone, turned to Jennifer and gave her directions to her mother's room. That meant she was still alive. Perhaps she had rallied, was getting better.

Jennifer made her way up the stairs, her hand on the smooth metal rail. Her legs were tired. When she reached the room, she saw Ross sitting beside the bed. He was asleep. The pale reddish hair was thinning rapidly, and his face was pasty and lifeless, as if he were the one on the point of death. His body sagged with sleep. He had a pot belly. He was only 34.

Jennifer looked toward her mother. Her face was yellow, and the skin was drawn so tight she looked like a skeleton. The features were a desperate parody of those Jennifer had known, and the body, which in her memory had always been soft and a little heavy, was small under the sheets. Jennifer stood in the doorway, convinced that she was too late, that her mother was dead. Her eyes blurred with tears, and she couldn't move into the room.

She wiped her eyes and saw a slight movement of breath. Her mother was alive. The tears returned, and she could not wipe them away. She let them come. She heard a tiny sound as one fell on the grey floor. At that moment, she was a child again, weeping and helpless, awaiting comfort from her mother, but the comfort wouldn't come. She could never ask for comfort again.

Jennifer stopped crying, wiped her eyes and moved to the side of the bed to touch Ross on the shoulder. His eyes opened, shocked; he shook his head and rubbed it with his hand.

"I couldn't stay awake."

"How is she?"

"No better. They're surprised she's lasted this long. She must have known."

"Can I talk to her?"

"She might be able to talk. Try and wake her."

Jennifer reached out and put her hand on her mother's arm. Her eyelids flickered but didn't open. Jennifer tightened the pressure of her hand a little. The eyes opened but stared ahead, unseeing.

"Mother."

The eyes shifted toward her.

"It's Jennifer."

Her mother recognized her and tried to smile, but the effort was greater than she could manage. Jennifer bent and kissed her.

"It's good to see you."

Her mother nodded. Jennifer took hold of the hand that lay on top of the covers and held it on her own. She was silenced now, there seemed nothing to say. The only subject that could be of interest to her mother was death, and Jennifer couldn't speak of that. The distance, the reticence was still overpowering.

"Has the minister been here?" she said to Ross.

"He was here for a few minutes last night, but she was asleep."

Ross looked frightened and confused, as if he was trying to keep too many things straight in his mind. Jennifer turned to her mother, determined to withhold nothing now, to offer whatever she could to the dying woman. Her mother's eyes met hers.

93

"Would you like me to pray?" Jennifer said. Her mother had attended church regularly all her life. Perhaps her belief was important to her. It was one of the things they had never discussed. She watched her mother's face for an answer to her question. At first she seemed not to have understood, but then she nodded her head.

Jennifer closed her eyes, held her mother's hand in hers and began to speak aloud. She hadn't said the words since she had left high school where every morning she had stood open-eyed and a little embarrassed praying to a God she no longer believed in. She was almost afraid she would forget the words, but they came easily. She held tight to the hand that was in her own, wishing for the old woman some sureness in the face of death. This is the body that bore me. This is the woman who kept me safe, as best she could, from the world's pain, though she understood me as little as I understood her.

Jennifer opened her eyes. She put down her mother's hand and got herself a chair, pulled it up close to the bed. The woman's breathing was heavier now. Her eyes were closed. Jennifer heard Ross stand up behind her.

"I'm going out to see if I can get a coffee," he said. "I'll be back in five minutes."

Jennifer nodded. She could hear the noises of morning activity beginning in the halls of the hospital. It would soon be time to phone the children. There was no way of knowing how long she'd have to stay here. Perhaps she could get Mrs. Buttle to move in for a day or so. She'd stayed overnight once before.

Her mother's breathing was heavier now, more laboured. Jennifer sat and held her hand and waited. From the moment of her arrival in the room, she had felt a surge of desperate energy, but now the lack of sleep was beginning to tell on her. Her eyes were heavy, and every muscle in her body ached. The moment in the bedroom came back, herself naked on the edge of the bed, Tom climbing out the

94

other side. Her mind was still at that moment.

She was startled awake by Ross' touch on her shoulder. She'd fallen asleep.

"Do you want to go to my place and sleep for a while? I can phone Dorothy."

"No. I'll stay for now. I have to phone the kids in a few minutes."

"There's a snack-bar open down the street if you want to get something."

Fresh air and a bite to eat might rouse her, but she didn't want to leave.

"I'll stay a little longer, then go out and phone and maybe get something."

"You might as well go now. She won't know you're gone."

There was an edge to his voice, almost of anger. Because she had come in from outside like the returned prodigal. Her mother's dying was properly his as the favourite son who'd stayed and whose life and family had been her mother's favourite interest. He was right. Jennifer was trying to make up for years of neglect with a dramatic presence at the moment of death. Ross had always been there.

Jennifer stood up to go. She left the hospital and walked down the quiet street. There was frost on the lawns, and the cold air seemed to pierce her clothing. She shivered as she walked and was glad to find that the snack-bar was close and overheated. She ordered coffee and toast.

There was something familiar about the man behind the counter. He had a long sallow face and bad teeth. She had gone to public school with him, in high school had lost track of him. He'd been a quiet, unobtrusive boy. She could see his face in an old class picture, sitting in the front row in a checked shirt, an uncomfortable grin on his face.

"You don't recognize me, Allan," she said to him when he brought the toast.

"Sure I do. You're Jenny Hopcroft."

95

"You didn't let on."

"I didn't suppose you'd remember me."

"You remembered me."

"That's different. I seen your picture in the paper and that. All the prizes you won."

"I'm not winning prizes any more."

What had made her say that? Some kind of exhaustion. As if she could only admit to this strange presence from the past how tired she was. Not just the trip up. Barbara. Eugene. Tom. The children. At this moment there was nothing inside her to meet all these demands. Allan stood still in front of her, his eyes nervously avoiding her as if he would have liked to run away.

"Is this your restaurant?"

"No. I just work here."

His face had a bleached look, like the clothes they'd worn as children that had gone through the wash too many times.

"I don't know if you heard, but for a while there I got to drinking. Lost everything I had, my car and all. Then I joined the AA and got straightened out and Gord, you remember Gord Cartwright, he took me on here."

Jennifer nodded. She didn't remember Gord. She was still struggling to remember Allan's last name, but it wouldn't come.

"You in town visiting?" he said.

"I drove up last night. My mother's in the hospital. She's dying."

"Maybe she'll come round. They can do wonderful things."

Jennifer shook her head.

"She's a nice lady, your mother. When I was drinking, I got so bad I was out on the street asking for money. I remember she came along one day, and she called me by name and gave me a real talking to. But nicely, you know. Then she gave me 50 cents and told me to go and get something to eat. Drunk as I was, I remembered that. After I got

96

myself straightened out, I always thought I'd like to go out to the house and just say hello and that I got myself right again."

Jennifer sipped her coffee and ate a bite of toast. She glanced at her watch.

"I have to phone home soon. I left in the middle of the night and my kids don't know I've gone."

Allan began to set things in order behind the counter. A man in a hard hat came in and ordered bacon and eggs. It was warm and comforting here, and Jennifer would have liked to dawdle over her coffee, but she must phone. She'd noticed a phone-booth outside the hospital. She finished and went to the cash register to pay.

"It's all right," Allan said. "You don't owe me anything."

"Of course I do."

"It's what I owe your mother," he said.

"All right."

She put out her hand, and he shook it.

"It's nice to see you again, Allan."

"You too."

Outside it seemed to have got colder. As she walked to the phone-booth, Jennifer couldn't stop shivering. Putting a coin in the slot, talking to the operator was laborious. It took great concentration not to stumble over words. The phone began to ring. It rang several times before Jennifer heard Cindy's sleepy voice on the other end.

"Cindy, it's Mum."

"Where are you?" Fear and confusion.

"At Grandma's. Uncle Ross phoned me last night to say Grandma was very sick. I drove up here in the middle of the night. There's a note downstairs."

"Is Grandma okay?"

"No, not really. I don't think she's going to get better."

There was a moment's silence. It was terrible to confront death like this, by long-distance telephone, yet this was the

97

way it happened now.

"I'll get Mrs. Buttle to come over."

"Are you coming back today?"

"I don't know. I'll phone Mrs. Buttle. You get ready for school."

"We don't have school. It's Remembrance Day."

"I forgot."

"Shall I phone Daddy?"

"Yes."

"Here's Gavin. Do you want to talk to him?"

"For a minute."

"Hi." Gavin's voice.

"I'm at Grandma's. She's in the hospital, very sick."

The euphemism bothered her now when she repeated it. Why did she not say simply, She's dying.

"We'll be okay," Gavin said.

"I'm going to phone Mrs. Buttle and Cindy's going to call Daddy. Can you find things to do all day?"

"Sure."

"Maybe Jeg could come over."

"Yeah."

"I better get back to the hospital now."

"Say Hi to Grandma."

She wondered whether Gavin had failed to understand that the old woman was dying or if he was only being brave and cheerful on principle. She said goodbye and hung up the phone. She called Mrs. Buttle, who was free that day and very kind and helpful in her officious way. She'd stay at the house until Jennifer returned. Jennifer called Irving.

"Take care of yourself," he said at the end of their short conversation and suddenly Jennifer had tears in her eyes, hung up the phone and began to sob, undermined and shaken by the simple and conventional kindness of it. Poor dumb human kindness.

Jennifer found a scrap of Kleenex in her coat pocket and wiped her eyes. She walked down the street to the hospital

98

feeling open and exposed, as if she were carrying her heart in her hand. Like something she remembered from a sonnet of Dante.

Allegro mi sembrava Amor tenendo
meo core in mano. . . .

The strength would come back. She must trust in that. But what if it didn't? Perhaps some people lived their lives in this state, raw to the touch. It was worse than any depression she'd ever experienced; that was a deadness, a spiritual sleep or hibernation. One waited for the spring to come.

A nurse was walking toward her down the street under the empty branches. She had a dark blue coat on over her uniform, but it was too short and the hem of her white uniform showed underneath. This nurse was another human being with perhaps a husband, children, parents dead or alive, the whole network of human complication was tied to her as well. Jennifer couldn't look at her.

She stood still to let the nurse go into the hospital ahead of her, then followed slowly up the steps and made her way back to her mother's room. Ross was staring out the window, his back to the bed. Her mother's breathing was louder, more strained.

"I met someone in the snack-bar that I used to go to school with."

"Al Kunelius?"

That was his last name. How could she have forgotten?

"You know him?"

"I used to hire him to unload a truck once in a while. Give him a couple of bucks for wine."

"He says he's joined AA and quit drinking."

"About time. He was getting to be a real pest. Turning up at the back door all the time. I finally had to get them to throw him in jail a couple of times. Then he stopped coming round."

99

The hardness sobered Jennifer and calmed her. She walked to the bed and took her mother's hand, but the woman was deep in unconsciousness.

Jennifer sat down in the chair beside the bed. There was nothing more to say or do. Only waiting. Her body ached. Images moved through her mind, images erotic and then grotesque; she tried to be rid of them and concentrate on her mother, but she couldn't reach her. No effort of will or imagination could take her further than to hold her hand. Tom surrounded her. He was an incubus, locked to her. He was not Tom in his separate human self, he was some destructive spirit tearing at her.

Jennifer's head jerked up, and she realized she had been dozing. She looked around the room. Ross stood in the corner looking toward her.

They sat for a slow eternity. Once a nurse walked in, looked toward them and then retreated. Again they waited, the woman's laboured breathing measuring the slow time and heavy silence. It went on. It went on.

Stopped.

There was no breathing. In the bed beside her, the woman had died. She held her mother's hand, but her mother had gone. She looked at the fingers, the thin silver wedding-band.

Jennifer put down her mother's hand and turned to Ross. There were tears in his eyes now as he looked down at the bed. This man, balding and growing fat, was the boy who had interrupted her life and pushed her into maturity. She put her arms around him, and for a moment they held each other.

"You'll come to the house," he said.

"I'd like to sleep for a while if I can. I'll have to go home and bring the kids back for the funeral."

"I'll make the arrangements."

He was looking toward the bed. Jennifer thought he must want to be alone with their mother, and it was surely his right, her youngest, favourite and most faithful child.

"I'll drive out to the house," she said, "and meet you there."

She walked out of the room and drew the door closed behind her. Outside, she looked at her watch. It was ten o'clock. She walked out of the hospital with a curious feeling of lightness, as if gravity had relaxed its pull on her. If she went to Ross's and slept for a few hours, she could drive back to Kingston in the evening. Tom could get his car back, and she could rent one to drive the children up for the funeral. There was so much to think of. Was it unfair of her to leave all the funeral arrangements to Ross? At least he was here, and Dorothy would take a certain officious delight in it all. She loved situations that allowed her to take charge. Jennifer didn't like Dorothy and Dorothy resented her on the grounds of her education, the fact that she had worked and travelled, and because she was divorced.

Jennifer stopped at the door of the car. The presence of death ought to be ennobling, to lift the eyes off petty things, but here she was walking away from her mother's death and delighting in spiteful thoughts about her sister-in-law. She tried to see Dorothy more generously, but without success. Dislike was not to be altered even by the spectre of eternity. Earth was powerful and recalcitrant.

Jennifer got in the car and put the keys in the ignition, then stopped as some pressure rose in her chest. The fact of her mother's death was all around her. She began to sob as if it would break her body. Grief shook her and shook her again. At last the sobbing eased. She must act, get into motion. She wiped her face, turned the key, pressed down on the gas pedal. The car moved.

To get to Ross's house, Jennifer had to drive through the centre of town, and as she passed the war memorial, she saw a few people beginning to gather. Her brother Harold's name was one of those engraved on the bronze plaque. Her father had always walked into town on November 11th and stood with the small crowd to hear the words spoken, the trumpet sound the Last Post. Jennifer remembered vividly standing there herself one cold sunny day, across the street from her father; for some reason they hadn't come together. Perhaps she had come with a group from the school. She heard the pleasant, slightly reedy voice of the Presbyterian minister begin the singing.

Oh God, our help in ages past,
our hope for years to come,
our shelter from the stormy blast,
and our eternal home. . . .

She had looked across at her father, at a certain painful stillness in the way he held his body, and she had tried to think of Harold.

She pulled the car to the side of the road and looked at the people gathered at the memorial. They were mostly older people, a couple of the men wearing Canadian Legion berets. A young trumpeter in an awkward dark suit was warming up the valves on his instrument.

Her mother never came to the service at the war memorial. Her reasons were never explained or discussed, and Jennifer wondered now what depths of bitterness her silence might have covered. Someone had made a war happen. Her son had gone to it. He had been killed, shot to death by another woman's son. Jennifer tried to imagine how she might feel if it had happened to Gavin. They were so brave, boys and young men, so absurdly brave in the face of an incomprehensible world. Harold had left school and gone to work because it was necessary. He had gone to war because it was right. He had walked ahead into gunfire.

Harold, her father, her mother. They were all lost. She couldn't conceive of a life beyond death, except now and then in a form of words so mysterious that for a moment she felt that all wonders were possible and true.

They are all gone into the world of light!
    And I alone sit ling'ring here;
Their very memory is fair and bright,
    And my sad thoughts doth clear.

She looked toward the memorial. A group of children
from the school arrived with a wreath to place when the
service started. In front was a girl, perhaps eleven, with a
serious face and long straight hair. She carried the wreath,
and there was a look of slight apprehension about her. She
was worried about walking forward with dignity and putting down the wreath, not having anything go wrong.
Jennifer felt vividly the little girl's concern, as if she were
inside her body, as if it were 25 years earlier and she were
standing watching her father across the street and hearing
the first words of the hymn.

My beloved dead. Gone into the world of light. If only
that, but it was inconceivable. It was too perfect, empty,
existence was not conceivable without the fret and pain,
meaningless. She knew the answer given. What is beyond
our apprehension is not therefore beyond God's. But the
words went dead, she could only cling to her loss and longing. She put her face in her hands and sat for a few minutes,
perfectly still, then raised her head and drove on to Ross's
house.

The drive was empty. Ross hadn't yet arrived. She could
see Dorothy peeking around the curtains in the front
window.

They met at the door.

"Ross phoned me," she said with a tragic air.

Jennifer just nodded.

"I remember I said to her last month she was looking
awful tired. I told Ross he better get her to the doctor, but
you know Ross, he didn't like to interfere."

"It might have been too late even then."

"When your time comes," Dorothy said.

"I guess so."

"Ross is downtown at McLaren and Fife's making the arrangements. They'll do a beautiful job. Young Tony McLaren's running the place now. Everybody comments that he does lovely funerals."

"Ross said I could sleep here for a while before I drive back."

"Are you going back right away? I thought maybe you could stay over. Kim and Julie can go in together and you can have Julie's room."

"I have to get back. I have to return the car, and I'll bring the kids."

"Not your car is it?"

Jennifer could sense an awakening interest in Dorothy's question. She was very alert to certain things.

"I rented it," Jennifer said.

She wouldn't have Dorothy speculating about her. Probably Dorothy knew that her statement was a lie, but it prevented more questions. She wouldn't have her knowing, even thinking about Tom. She would keep him safe from that.

"A nice car," Dorothy said, frustrated by the dead end.

"I'm exhausted," Jennifer said. "Could I just sleep now?"

"Sure. Poor Jenny. Come into Kim's room. I sent the kids out for a while when I heard you were coming over so it would be quiet enough for you. Kim's is the best bed. If I want a little nap in the afternoon, I always sneak into Kim's bed. It's real cosy."

She led Jennifer up the stairs and down the hall to her eldest daughter's room. It was a conventional little girl's room with the beginnings of adolescence superimposed. Kim was only a year younger than Cindy. There was a poster of Mick Jagger sweating and sneering, and over the bed the four Beatles. On the other wall was someone Jennifer didn't recognize. In the corner of the room was a small record-player with a pile of records beside it. The bed had pink flounces hanging from the mattress to the floor and on the table beside it lay a pile of Archie comic-books and a tube of lipstick.

"Just make yourself at home," Dorothy said as she pulled down the blind of the one window. "Do you want a cup of tea or anything?"

"No. Thank you."

"We'll see you later."

She left the room, drawing the door closed behind her. Jennifer sat on the bed and took off her shoes. She wiggled her toes to relax the tension in her feet. As she took off her clothes, she went back again to the moment last night when she had put them on in her own bedroom with Tom moving around her, the bed wet from their loving. If only Tom were here. He would hold her as she slept. She pulled down the covers on the bed and got in. It was wonderful to close her eyes.

She thought of the poster on the wall over her. *Ringo, George, Paul and John, bless the bed that I lie on.* She giggled at her own silliness, curled deeper into the bed, pulled the covers over her head. She thought of her mother's body abused by embalmers. Perhaps she ought to have objected. No, it was right to leave it to Ross, whatever his intentions. You had to let go.

She drifted into a sound sleep. When she woke she had been dreaming about Barbara Walker. It was some sort of a circus, and she was tied to a telephone-pole and a crowd was throwing things at her. She was bruised and bleeding, but when Jennifer tried to make them stop, they redoubled their efforts. Jennifer opened her eyes. She was confused, lost in time and space. It wasn't clear where she was or what day this was. She looked at her watch. It was four in the afternoon. She must get up and drive back to Kingston. As she got out of bed, and put on her clothes, she realized that Cindy and Gavin didn't yet know her mother was dead.

She must phone and let them know she'd be home. She could tell them then.

Or would it be better to wait until she got home? No, she'd tell Cindy on the phone, better to have it done. Jennifer went to the bathroom and splashed her face with water. Her mouth felt dry and unpleasant, and she wished she had a toothbrush. There was an ache in her shoulder, and she felt only half-refreshed by the sleep. She took a drink of cold water from a glass by the sink and rinsed it around her mouth.

Dorothy was waiting for her downstairs. She must go down. As she walked out the door of the bathroom, she saw a small figure in a dark corner at the end of the hall. Reddish hair, a round serious face peering out of the dark corner, catching just enough light to show the small features. The eyes were observant, concentrated.

It was Ross at eight years old. The delusion was momentary, but it shook Jennifer, sent echoes through the empty space left by her mother's death.

"Hi Jimmy," she said when she could rouse herself to speak.

"Hi," he said and turned and disappeared into an adjacent bedroom.

She hadn't seen her nephew for a couple of years, and he had grown and changed. As she went down the stairs, she wondered if he had always looked that much like Ross or if it was a trick of the light.

Dorothy was in the kitchen making a glass of chocolate milk for Julie, a rather plain little girl lost behind a pair of heavy glasses.

"I told you you were going to lose it if you weren't more careful," Dorothy was saying. "Well you're not getting another one."

She turned when she heard Jennifer.

"Did you have a good sleep, Jenny?"

"Yes."

"Ross came in after you went up. He looked just awful. I tried to get him to lie down, but he wouldn't. He's gone off somewhere in the car."

"I met Jimmy upstairs. He looks a lot like Ross at that age."

"That's what your mother always said." She put the glass of milk down in front of Julie. "Has the cat got your tongue, Julie? Aren't you going to say hello to Aunt Jenny?"

"Hello Aunt Jenny."

"Hi Julie. Did you get the card Gavin made for your birthday?"

"Julie, don't just nod. You've got a tongue in your head, use it," Dorothy said.

"Could I use the telephone?" Jennifer said.

"You can use the extension up in our bedroom if you want privacy."

"I just want to tell Gavin and Cindy that I'll be home tonight."

"You're sure you won't stay over?"

"I really can't."

It was Cindy's voice that answered the call.

"Hello love," Jennifer said. "I just phoned to tell you I'll be home tonight."

There was a moment's hesitation before Cindy spoke. She knew.

"How's Grandma?"

"She died this morning. There was nothing anyone could do."

Again there was a pause as Cindy gathered herself together.

"Are you okay, Mummy?" she said.

Jennifer's eyes blurred with tears.

"Yes I'm fine. I'll see you in a little while."

"I haven't been able to get hold of Daddy yet. I'm just going over to his office."

"I'll be home before you're asleep. Is Gavin there?"

"He's out somewhere with Jeg. Shall I tell him about Grandma?"

"Yes, I guess so."

"Drive carefully."

"I will."

Jennifer put down the phone. She looked around her at the gilt mirror, the ornate hall table. She wanted to get out of this strange place and back to her own home, not even to have to say goodbye, just to go straight out the door now. She turned and went toward the kitchen.

Julie had disappeared, and Dorothy was peeling potatoes.

"I think I'll go now. I'll come back up the day after tomorrow. The funeral will be Friday, I imagine."

"You'll have something to eat, won't you? I'm just making supper."

Jennifer hesitated. All her habits and training told her to be polite and stay for dinner.

"I really couldn't eat anything," she said. In fact she was hungry, but it seemed that lying to Dorothy was becoming a habit. It was easy, almost enjoyable.

"You must have something."

Why was Dorothy determined to make her eat? Was it kindness or convention or simply a blind insistence on having her own way?

"Maybe I could take an apple or something. In case I get hungry in the car."

"You're sure you won't stay for a bite of supper? I can have it done in no time at all."

"No, Dorothy, really. I don't feel like eating."

Dorothy opened the fridge and took out an apple.

"It's a terrible thing. She wasn't really an old woman. She always seemed full of beans. We used to go out on Sundays with the children, she always liked that." She sighed. "Well Jenny, I guess you've got your own life to live there in Kingston."

"Thanks for everything," Jennifer said with as much hypocritical friendliness as she could manage. Anything to get out. Dorothy walked with her to the door, and when they got there hugged her. Jennifer objected silently, and in some part of her mind wondered if she was being unfair.

As the car moved away from the house, she felt relief, but within a few miles she began to feel that the drive was long and that she hadn't slept enough to manage it. She stopped once for a hamburger, but by the time she saw the lights of Kingston and pulled off Highway 401, her body ached, and she was gripping the steering-wheel with weary desperation. As she climbed out of the car in front of her house, she felt slightly nauseated, wanted to collapse into a warm bath, drink a bottle of beer and go to bed.

Mrs. Buttle met her at the door. There was a look of concern on her face. Behind her, Cindy came racing down the stairs, fully dressed.

"Daddy's in the hospital," she said. "When I went to his office this afternoon, they'd just heard that he was taken to the hospital this morning."

Jennifer felt that she was gasping for air. She tried to calm herself, to breathe slowly.

"What's the matter with him?"

Mrs. Buttle spoke.

"They couldn't tell Cindy much so I phoned the hospital. Apparently a perforated ulcer, and he's been haemorrhaging. They had to operate this afternoon."

"Is he all right?"

"You know how they are. Won't tell you anything."

"I want to see him," Cindy said.

Gavin appeared from his room.

"You hear about Dad?"

"Yes."

She took off her coat, trying to make sense of it all, to make a decision as to what should be done. Her mind was empty. She seemed unable to think. She knew this called for a response, but for the moment she only felt detached and irritable. She wanted to escape from it.

"Can we go to the hospital now?"

"It's long past visiting hours."

What if Robert died? He couldn't die. He had always been there. For so many years. But he neglected himself. He'd ignored the warnings, to punish himself and her. Jennifer walked to the sink and poured a glass of water.

"Can I make you something?" Mrs. Buttle said. "You must be worn out."

"I don't think I could get anything down."

They were all looking at her, expecting a response, a decision. If only she could be alone for a couple of minutes. She made an excuse and went toward the bathroom, locked herself inside, stood in front of the mirror and then put her head against the cool surface.

She urinated, washed her hands, dawdled. Began to be able to think a little. She must do something to reassure Cindy and Gavin. Go to the hospital, even if it was late. Back into that other world of life and death.

Before Barbara's phone call, she hadn't been in a hospital since Gavin's birth in England. Now she was beginning to feel that she lived in them. The strange atmosphere was becoming like home. She emerged from the bathroom and went down to where they waited for her.

"I'm going down to the hospital," she said.

"I want to come," Cindy said.

"No. Not when it's so late. I'll just see what I can find out. If I go alone, they're more likely to let me see him. I'll come right back and let you know how he is, and you can go tomorrow."

Cindy was looking sulky.

"You could take me if you wanted to."

"You can go tomorrow."

"He could die, and I'd never even see him."

"He's not going to die."

"You don't even care."

"Don't be like that."

It was a mechanical response. She was too dead to do more, though beneath the deadness, that sleepwalker's slowness, she knew there was a fury that would like to strike the child. Cindy turned and walked noisily up the stairs.

"I'll stay here until you're back," Mrs. Buttle was saying.

Jennifer went out and started down the street to the hospital. A cold wind blew at her back.

> The north wind shall blow
> And we shall have snow
> And what shall cock robin do then, poor thing?

Her father had sung that to her sometimes. At night when she was in her bed cuddled up against the cold in the room that she and Ross shared for a couple of years, warmed only a little by the curve of black stove pipe that came through the floor and up to the chimney.

> He'll hide in the barn
> And keep himself warm
> And hide his head under his wing, poor thing.

Poor Robert. Alone here, she could begin to sense his existence, the pain as the ulcer ate its bitter way through his flesh. He would hold it in silence. He must be very lonely.

When she reached the hospital and asked the location of his room, the receptionist told her that visiting hours were over. So did the nurse as she approached the nursing-station. She semed an irascible woman, and Jennifer was afraid she'd get nothing from her. The only way, she decided, was to let herself seem totally vulnerable. She knew that with her pale complexion and shadowed eyes it was an impression she created easily. Speak softly and carry a big tear.

"I've been out of town. My mother just died," she said to the woman. "We're divorced, but the children are very upset. They just heard late this afternoon. I said I'd come over and see what I could find out."

The woman looked down at her sheets of paper. Jennifer had left her no room for anger.

"He was in surgery this afternoon. He's resting now."

"I understand he was haemorrhaging."

"He's had three transfusions."

"Can you tell me what the surgery was?"

"I believe they removed a section of the stomach."

She wouldn't look at Jennifer. She stared at Robert's chart and tidied away a few loose papers. Jennifer stood in silence, willing the woman to look up and meet her eyes. The silence extended itself painfully. Finally the woman glanced toward her.

"Can I see him? Just for a moment?"

"I suppose it's all right, but from now on you'll have to come during visiting hours."

"Yes. I know."

The nurse conducted her down the bare hall. Jennifer couldn't quite believe that it was only a few hours since she'd walked down another hospital hallway to her mother's room. That seemed like another lifetime. The nurse led her into a room with an open door.

There was a tube in his arm from the intravenous, another tube from the abdomen. The skin of his face was pale and grey. The body was passive, awkward, unreal in the hospital gown.

Robert's eyes opened, took in her presence. He smiled. She went and stood beside the bed.

"How are you?" she said.

"Okay. I'll be okay. Full of dope and antibiotics."

"I just heard. Cindy's terribly worried. I was away. My mother died."

"Sorry."

His eyes closed, tried to open.

"I'm dopey."

His words were slurred a little.

"I'll let you get back to sleep. The kids will be in to see you tomorrow."

He opened his eyes again with an effort.

"Thanks. For coming."

She nodded to him and left the room, still vibrating with an awareness of his damaged body. A body she had once shared. The first man to touch her, one night in a borrowed apartment, the first to enter her.

They had excised part of his stomach. They had cut him and sewed him back together.

Walking home, Jennifer tried to make plans for the rest of the week, tomorrow then the trip up, but her mind slid over details without getting any purchase on them. She must sleep first, then make plans. Back at the house, she thanked Mrs. Buttle and paid her for her time. It took nearly the last of her cash.

"Is Daddy really all right?" Cindy said as soon as Mrs. Buttle was out the door.

"Yes. You can go and see him tomorrow."

"What did they do to him?" Gavin said.

"They took out a piece of his stomach that was perforated by an ulcer."

"Yuck."

"How does he look?" Cindy said.

"Pretty sick, but he'll be getting stronger from now on."

The phone rang.

"You two get off to bed," Jennifer said. "I'll come up and cover you in a few minutes."

She picked up the phone. When she heard Tom's voice, she was almost speechless with thanks and pleasure.

"I wasn't sure you'd be back."

"She died this morning . . . it doesn't feel like this morning, I slept for a while in the afternoon, and I don't know what day it is any more."

"You must be exhausted."

"Isn't there a stronger word than that? I got back and discovered Robert's in the hospital with a perforated ulcer. They operated this afternoon."

"Is he all right?"

"I think so. Cindy's going to be in a bit of a state until she sees him, but she can go tomorrow."

"What about the funeral?"

"It's Friday. But I've promised myself I won't start thinking about anything until I've had some sleep. How are you?"

"I'm fine."

"Are you coming to get the car?"

"I have a meeting. I can't come until about eleven. Can you stay up that long?"

"I don't know. I want to see you. . . . No, I better sleep. Can I see you tomorrow?"

"Let's meet for lunch."

"Okay."

"I thought of coming over tonight. . . ."

Jennifer hesitated, wondered if she could sleep in a chair until eleven. Her head was aching and she had chills.

"I'd be boring," she said. "I'm just too tired."

"I'll pick you up at 12.30."

"I can't wait."

"Go to bed now. Sleep tight."

"Goodnight Tom."

"Goodnight."

Jennifer hung up. She wanted him here, now. She made her way to the kitchen where Bena was crouched in the corner eating the last of a bowl of catfood. She would make herself a cup of hot milk.

5

Jennifer stared at the girl who stood close in front of her, her face hard and stubborn.

"Of course you have to go to the funeral."

"I won't."

"I don't suppose anybody likes funerals. . . ."

"I don't want to go away while Daddy's sick."

"It will only be for a couple of days."

"He could die."

"Oh Cindy . . ."

"He could."

"Don't be silly, he'll be all right. You saw him this morning."

"He looks awful. I'm not going."

"You have to."

"You don't care what happens to Daddy, but I do."

"Don't be ridiculous."

"You don't care because you have a new boyfriend."

"That's enough of that."

"You probably want him to die."

Jennifer grabbed Cindy by the shoulders and shook her. Though Cindy was taller, Jennifer's anger gave her sufficient strength that the girl's body seemed light and limp. She shook her hard. Cindy's eyes were frightened but defiant. Jennifer let go of her and turned away, stunned by the energy of her own rage. She could feel the anger still ready to break out again.

"I'm not going."

"The woman was my mother. You're not going to insult her."

"He's my father."

"You can see him when you come back. He's not going to die."

"You don't know."

Jennifer could feel the anger growing again. It was almost uncontrollable, and worse, felt justified. Nothing was so blind and dangerous as righteous anger. She must do away with that terrible sense of justification. Was Cindy right? Could she secretly be hostile to Robert, pleased with the idea of being rid of him? No. No. But she saw a gleam of light.

"Look," she said. "You go to the hospital and ask him what you should do."

There was a sulky silence.

"He'll say to go to the funeral," she said at last.

"Yes he will."

Cindy was unable to find a response. Jennifer could sense the electricity in the air around her. Cindy's body was stiff. It looked awkward, grotesque. She breathed in suddenly, began to cry.

"All right, I'll go."

Jennifer was still angry and wounded, but she went to Cindy and put her arm around her.

"I have some idea how you feel Cindy. I'm sure you cared about Grandma, and I know you care about your father."

"He could die, you know. He looks terrible."

"Yes, he looks very sick, but now that they've operated, he'll get stronger. He won't die. We'll come back as soon as we can after the funeral, and you can go and see him."

"I guess so," Cindy said. She drew away and walked out of the bedroom.

"I'll come and see you in bed," Jennifer said. She went and sat down on the edge of her own bed. She'd won, but it gave her no satisfaction. She could feel the beginnings of a headache, and she rubbed her temples. She returned resentfully to Cindy's remark about Tom and Robert. She had tried with Robert, damn it, done everything she could to save the marriage; now she had a right to something else.

Lunch with Tom had been marvellous. Once or twice, as

116

they sat there holding hands under the table, Jennifer had felt guilty that she wasn't overcome with sorrow for her mother, but she couldn't help the happiness, undutiful or not; she felt good, ate well and talked feverishly. Once or twice she'd seen Tom's eyes move toward friends or acquaintances who came into the place, but he didn't withdraw. He was too careless, but it pleased her. Within that precise, controlled exterior was an impulsive warm man. That was how she thought of him, warm, solid, radiating heat. He said it made him sound like an old iron cookstove, and she agreed.

Jennifer kicked off her shoes and put a pillow against the head of the bed and leaned against it, her feet stretched out in front of her. She wiggled her toes and looked around the room. On the opposite wall was a Rouault print. Robert had given it to her when he returned after his period in the therapeutic community. It was from the *Miserere* series, a portrait of an abused Christ, his head turned down, the crown of thorns suggesting a halo.

She hadn't looked at the print for a long time, not with real attention. She'd lost the capacity to respond to the power and amplitude of the image. For a moment now, she could. And yet a few minutes before, she'd been in a rage with Cindy. She was all in pieces. There was joy in her feeling for Tom, and yet an intense selfishness as well. Could they live together with the children? She didn't want to share him with anyone, not even with Gavin and Cindy. She didn't want them to make demands on him.

In the morning when she woke, there was brilliant sunshine outside her window, and the sun held for the whole trip. The woods at the edge of the road were rich with warm browns, russet, umber and ochre, earth colours warmed by sunlight. Gavin sat in front beside her while in the back seat Cindy read, then curled up to sleep.

The car grew quite hot as it moved along in the sunlight, and the lake was brilliant blue when it came in sight, but when they reached the motel where Jennifer had made reservations, it was late afternoon, and the air was almost cold.

"There's a nip in the brook," Gavin said, quoting from a children's story that had been a favourite of his.

"There certainly is."

There was a double bed in the room for her and Cindy, and the manager moved in a cot for Gavin. When they'd taken a few minutes to settle, they drove to Ross's house. Dorothy had wanted them to stay there, but Jennifer knew that she'd be more patient if she had a place where she and the children could get away on their own. At the time of her father's funeral, she'd been angered at what then seemed to her a barbaric ritual, offended at the commonplaces of neighbours and acquaintances, hurt by the need to go through empty gestures. It had been an assault on her love and grief. Older now, she was prepared to accept the necessity of it all, but it wouldn't be easy to be told how beautiful the corpse looked, to pretend to know people she couldn't remember, to deflect Dorothy's veiled hostility.

When they arrived at the house, Ross wasn't there.

"He's down at the home," Dorothy said, "to meet those who come to pay their respects. He thought maybe you could go down for a while after supper."

"Of course."

"Cindy's getting tall, isn't she? Takes after Robert."

Julie appeared on the stairs.

"Hi Gavin," she said.

The two of them were of an age and had become friendly on visits when Jennifer and Robert were living in Toronto.

"Julie, you take Gavin and Cindy upstairs and find something nice for them to do. Tell Kim to come out of her room."

Cindy's eyes glanced toward Jennifer, looking for an excuse to stay with the adults.

"Kim's got quite a collection of records," Jennifer said.

"I had a sleep in her room when I was here."

Cindy's mouth tightened, and she went off up the stairs after the others. Dorothy led the way into the kitchen.

"An awful lot have come to the home," Dorothy said. "Ross has been there all the time. Ted and Irene came last night to give him a rest, but he stayed on anyhow."

"How's Ted?" Jennifer hadn't seen her cousin in years. He was older than she was, almost Harold's age, in fact the two had been close friends growing up.

"He wasn't looking too good for a while there, but then he had his operation—gallstones—and ever since then he's been looking wonderful. He's a grandfather now."

"Really?"

"Nancy and Darryl had a little girl last winter."

"That's a shock."

"Be you or me next. I'll bet Cindy has all kinds of boyfriends. She's real cute."

"She's a bit young."

"Kim's been going out with Charlie Englehart's boy. Just to the show, things like that. Nothing serious."

The terrible race to have a boyfriend, to be settled. Dorothy had felt it for herself, now for her children. When Jennifer had come back from England for her father's funeral, Ross was only seventeen, still in high school, but Dorothy had staked her claim. Younger than he was, a little chubby, hardly having lost her baby fat, it seemed, yet she and Ross were like an old married couple. She organized and hectored and bemoaned his failings. She'd changed little since, except that the lines of her face and figure had hardened, and the streak of hurt angry malevolence was stronger, seemed more in danger of escaping its bounds. In the past, its main force of expression was a fierce frugality, a persistent war on waste, but it was closer to the surface now, it seemed to show its face behind all her words.

"What does the doctor say about Robert?"

"They seem to think he'll be all right. Cindy's been very

worried about him."

"Does it bother them a lot, the two of you not being together?"

"They seem to be able to deal with it."

"Probably you're better off without him anyways. Always on his high horse, wasn't he?"

"I wouldn't say that."

Robert had always made an attempt to be accommodating when they came to visit. Not that he could ever emulate Ross's defeated air. Jennifer wanted to say that, but there was no point. To fight Dorothy, you had to meet her on her own ground—she recognized no other—and on her own territory under ancient rules that she knew by instinct, she was invincible. How would she deal with Tom? His position as a judge, for one thing, would force her to take him seriously. And Tom was solid, substantial. Not to underrate Dorothy. Talk about Tom's daughter, that would soften him up. How would he feel about her if he left? Perhaps it was absurd to think he ever would.

"Ross said he'd come back for some supper about five," Dorothy said as she stood up and went to the counter. She took up a plastic bag of carrots, slit it neatly open with a paring knife and began to scrape and cut.

"Can I help with anything?" Jennifer said.

"Oh no. No need of that."

Cindy appeared at the kitchen doorway. Dorothy looked toward her. Another one on her high horse, the look said. Jennifer was embarrassed. Why in hell couldn't Cindy stay with her cousins?

"Are you going to come to the funeral home tonight?" Jennifer said.

"What for?"

"To meet the people who come and thank them for coming."

Cindy looked puzzled. It was a choice between that and staying with her cousins.

"I guess I'll come."

Dorothy was silent. Jennifer had won a point on Cindy's choice of the adult role. Even if she didn't have a boyfriend. Cindy sat down at the table, and there was a heavy silence as Dorothy put on the carrots and a pot of potatoes.

"Too bad about your father, Cindy," Dorothy said as she turned around. "I don't know what Kim would do if anything like that ever happened to Ross. She's her father's girl, that's for sure."

Jennifer was afraid that Cindy was about to cry.

"Who's conducting Mother's funeral?" she said.

"Reverend Irwin."

"Would I know him."

"No, I don't think so. He's just been at the church here a couple of years. Nice man, though his wife's not all she should be. Several people in the congregation aren't speaking to her."

There was the sound of a car in the driveway. Dorothy looked out the kitchen window.

"He looks worn out," she said.

The front door opened, and Ross made his way to the kitchen.

"You've got to get a proper sleep, Ross," Dorothy said as he entered the room. "Get some pills from Dr. Strauss if you can't do it any other way. You look like death warmed over."

Ross ignored the lecture, said hello to Jennifer and Cindy.

"You can have a lie-down after supper."

"I said I'd be back by 6.30."

"I'll go tonight," Jennifer said. "You can take a break."

"I might as well go along with you," Ross said. "Ted and Irene won't be there tonight. There's something on at Kelly's school."

"Cindy and I can manage."

"He won't let you go alone," Dorothy said. "Has to look after it all. I've given up trying to talk sense to him. He did everything for her when she was alive."

She took out a pile of dinner plates and moved toward the dining-room with them. Jennifer looked at her brother. His skin was grey against the dark colour of his suit. His hair seemed even thinner than it had two days ago. There was something in his eyes that made her wonder if he might have been drinking.

Dorothy announced dinner. The children sat at the kitchen table, the three adults in the dining-room. The food was good, and Jennifer wondered if she had been unfair to Dorothy in remembering her as a poor cook. Perhaps she'd just been slow to learn.

Dorothy kept up a desultory harangue through the meal, selected subjects having to do with Ross's minor flaws. Once or twice the subject of the store came up, and there was an edge to her voice somehow, a tone that Jennifer couldn't quite place. She wondered if there was some problem with the business. It was an office-supply store where Ross had gone to work after Grade 12. Jim Truax, the owner, was getting on in years, and when he was ready to retire, Ross had made an arrangement to run the store and gradually to buy it. The business was successful enough that it was a good arrangement for both of them. Jennifer suspected that Mrs. Truax still owned a bit of the store, but unless the business had fallen off disastrously, there should be no problem there.

Ross ate stolidly, not replying to any of Dorothy's remarks. Jennifer listened for the sounds of the children's voices and hoped that Cindy was making an effort to be friendly. Why did she care about Dorothy's unspoken accusation that Jennifer's children were "spoiled"? The small town assumption that the worst of maternal sins, worse than being a poor housekeeper, was to spoil your children, meaning to take them and their feelings seriously. Dorothy hadn't been "spoiled," that was clear, and the reservoirs of rancour were bottomless.

Jennifer heard Gavin's voice, once or twice thought she heard a couple of words from Cindy. Sometimes she wondered where Gavin had learned or inherited his gregariousness and high spirits. Perhaps from her father, there had been that in him, though suppressed by restraints imposed by family and circumstance.

After dinner, she and Cindy went to the motel to change their clothes for the funeral parlour, leaving Gavin with his cousins.

As they walked out of the cold starry night into the motel room, the heat was at first pleasant and then oppressive.

"Will you be all right at the funeral home?" Jennifer said.

"What's it like?"

"It's hard. The coffin's open, and people come to see her. It's a strange custom, I suppose. I used to think it was dreadful. At my father's funeral I hated it, but I suppose it has some importance. It helps people to accept the fact of death."

"It sounds creepy."

"If you can't manage, just leave quietly. You can wait in a restaurant or something."

"I'll be okay."

"I'm going to have a shower."

"Can I phone Daddy at the hospital?"

"I don't know if he has a telephone in his room."

"Can I try?"

"All right."

Jennifer went into the small bathroom and took off her clothes. She pinned up her hair and put on a plastic shower-cap.

The water poured over her. She turned to let it strike the tense muscles of her shoulders. Aware of her body, she wanted Tom, soaped her skin and longed for him to be with her. When she turned off the water, the air was cold on her skin. Reality. He was married to someone else. She would have to steal him; she didn't want to do that.

As Jennifer came out of the bathroom, Cindy was standing in her underwear by the mirror brushing her hair. She was so slender and graceful. She was a woman. Jennifer felt for a moment that she could tell her about Tom.

"Daddy's fine," Cindy said. "He says he'll be out of the hospital in another few days."

"Good."

Jennifer turned away to dress herself, as if to hide her heavy old vulnerable body from this lovely uncaring child. She covered herself with clothes that were unobtrusive, conventional for a time like this. Let Cindy be beautiful; she herself would be invisible.

"Remember to go to the bathroom before we leave," she said.

Cindy gave her a look and did up the last button on the dark grey tweed skirt. Jennifer brushed out her hair and put it in a bun on the back of her head. There was a quiet hiss from the heating system that kept the room too hot for comfort. They'd have to sleep with the window open.

Cindy put on her coat and sat on the edge of the bed waiting while Jennifer put on a little eye makeup. Jennifer was afraid she might cry at the funeral home and make a mess of it, but as she was launched, she resolved not to cry and went on. The makeup would make her look a little less naked.

They drove without speaking to the undertaker's stone building on the main street. As she was parking, she recognized Ross's car nearby, glad that he was there ahead of them, that there would be a familiar face.

As they entered the dim room containing the coffin, Jennifer saw Cindy flinch and pull back. Ross took their coats, and Jennifer looked at her daughter and then walked toward the body. It looked, as they always looked, younger, more placid and still than in life. She wondered if Tony

McLaren supervised all the details. She remembered him from school as a dirty-minded little sneak.

Jennifer took Cindy's hand in the hope that it might help. Ross stood a little away from them. Her mother's face was quite beautiful. Cindy was perhaps more like her than Jennifer had ever realized. For all her resolution not to cry, Jennifer now found herself on the edge of tears. She turned her face toward her daughter whose features were strained and flushed. It was her first look at human death. It wouldn't be fair to her if Jennifer cried. She bit her lip hard and breathed deeply. The tears went away.

She led Cindy away from the coffin.

"Are you all right?"

Cindy gave a tight desperate shake of the head.

"Do you want to go?"

"For a minute."

"Just go out and walk around for a while."

Cindy nodded and took her coat.

"Pretty hard for a kid," Ross said as she walked out of the room.

"Pretty hard for anybody."

Jennifer looked at the book to be signed by those who came to visit.

"Many people been in?"

"A lot."

Jennifer went to the book and looked through the names. Most were familiar though it wasn't often she could remember faces. Some were names of people she remembered as children, Ross' friends, she assumed. At the bottom of one page, in large, almost childish handwriting, was the name Allan Kunelius. He was left-handed, Jennifer remembered, and had always had an awkward manner of writing, his whole body turned almost in a knot to get a hand on the page. And he always wore rubber boots, winter and summer.

As she moved away from the book, someone came through the door. It was an older woman, a retired schoolteacher that her mother had known through the W. I. Ross went to meet her, shook her hand and spoke for a moment, accompanied her to the body. Jennifer turned away.

She wondered where Cindy was, whether she'd come back. It was cold for her to sit in the car. Jennifer thought perhaps she should go and drive her back to Dorothy's or the motel.

There was another figure at the doorway. She turned and was startled to recognize Attler Woodie. She'd assumed he must be dead. He seemed old even in her childhood when she saw him every day sitting on the bench outside the town hall, mud and manure on his rubber boots, a cigarette or sometimes a cheap cigar hanging from his lips. He had been a phenomenon, a feature of the landscape like the old horse-watering trough, inexplicable, then not needing explanation after a while because he was always there. Someone had once said he was a remittance-man, and as a child, Jennifer thought that had something to do with taxes. She'd never known, once she was old enough to understand the expression, whether it was true or not. Attler had a shack on the edge of town with a stovepipe sticking out of the roof and an old bus-driver's seat outside the door. His walk was aimless and shambling, now and then a drunken totter. For most of the year he could be found on the bench outside the town hall, a figure almost comic, but just formidable enough that the local children liked to stay on the good side of him.

Jennifer walked to the door to meet him. The pupils of his eyes were ringed with white. There was a smell of age and tobacco and urine and, she would have sworn, horses, though surely there were none left around his shack.

She could see Ross looking toward her, his face rigid. He wanted Attler out of here.

The old man had done his best to dress up. He had on a tie that didn't match his plaid shirt and a pair of black Oxfords that contrasted strangely with the brown trousers

126

worn shiny. His head was nearly bald now, and the skin was papery. He seemed like a man out of another age, out of her childhood, when the town was full of mysteries.

Jennifer reached out and shook his hand.

"I'm Jenny Hopcroft, Attler. I'm glad you could come."

His eyes made an effort to get her clear.

"I remember. You used to win the prizes down at the school."

"Some of them."

His eyes moved toward the coffin. Ross and the old schoolteacher were moving away now, and she could see Ross watching out of the corner of his eye. He wanted to come over, take charge, get Attler quickly out of the way lest someone respectable come in and find him here. The town wasn't a mine of memories to Ross, it was the locus of his daily life, and it must be kept in order.

"She looks lovely," Attler was saying as they came to her mother's body. "She was always a lovely girl. I kind of had my heart set on her once, when she was just a little thing. I used to see her coming downtown on Saturdays. She was just a girl then, I was back from France. From the war. I used to talk to her. She was a bit frightened of me, I guess. They used to tell stories about me. I'd see her when she came downtown, and I'd tell her that I was going to be her beau when she got a bit older." He turned to Jenny and smiled. He hadn't many teeth left. "She thought it was all a joke, but she was the loveliest little thing I ever saw." His voice faded. "Just a girl then."

His voice was high and thin, but it was without the peculiar edge she remembered in it from the days when he sat on the bench and talked to those who went by. The sense of performance, that's what was missing. She realized now that for years he'd been playing a role. It was a shock to hear the plainness of his voice now, the sad truthfulness. He stood looking down for a long moment. Ross was watching from the door.

"The loveliest little thing I ever saw. Do you think I could give her a . . . a little kiss?"

His voice was soft as he said it, but Ross heard him from his place at the door. He started to move toward them, but Jennifer looked toward him and shook her head. He stopped.

"I think it would be all right," she said. "I think she'd be pleased."

Attler lifted his arm to his face and wiped his lips one at a time on the sleeve of his sweater, then bent and kissed the still lips lightly, stood and turned away.

"Thank you very much," he said.

"I'm glad you could come."

Jennifer walked to the door with him and saw him out. When she turned back into the room, Ross avoided her eyes.

"I'm going out to see where Cindy is," she said. She went down the hall to the street. The cold air made her shiver as she looked up and down the street without seeing any sign of her daughter. She went across to the car, but Cindy wasn't there either. She was about to go back in when she saw Cindy appear around a corner and walk toward her. She went past the hardware and a new snack-bar to meet her.

"Are you okay?" she said.

"I think so. I'll come back in now."

"Are you sure?"

"Yes. I'll be fine."

She said it with angry insistence, determined to have control of herself. As they reached the door of the funeral parlour, they met John and Shirley Chivers, old acquaintances of her mother from the church. She introduced Cindy to them, and they talked with a certain placid acceptance of the death. Inside the room with them, everything seemed more ordinary, and when a handful of other people arrived shortly after, the time was taken up with civilities.

Groups arrived, made their awkward pilgrimage to the

128

coffin, signed the book, and left. Three times Ross excused himself and went to the toilet. He must be going out for a drink, Jennifer decided. Not surprising after what he must have been through the last few days.

When the time set for visiting was over, the three of them came silently out to the street. Down at the next corner, two boys were shoving each other back and forth across the sidewalk.

"Watch it, you prick."

"What's the matter, fag?"

"Piss off."

Ross went to his car; Jennifer and Cindy made their way to theirs.

At the house, Ross offered her a drink, and Jennifer accepted with pleasure. She noticed that the drink he made himself was mostly whisky. Booze was as good a way as any to get through the experience of a death. Jennifer took a long drink of the rye and ginger ale he'd made her and sank into the chair. It seemed that within seconds the effect of the alcohol went through her tense and tired body, making her all the more aware of the knots of muscle in her back and shoulders. She drank again to loosen them.

Gavin came to the door of the living-room. She raised her hand to wave to him, and when he came to her chair, put out an arm and hugged him.

"Having a good time?"

"Pretty good."

He sat down on the floor beside her chair. Cindy came into the room with Dorothy right behind her, Cindy crossing the whole width of the room to avoid her aunt's pursuit and sitting on a straight chair that stood away from the other furniture. Dorothy stopped in the middle of the room and looked around her.

"Well," she said. "Where are *my* children?"

"They're all right where they are," Ross said. "Do you want a drink?"

"Since everyone else seems to be indulging, I suppose I might as well."

When Ross came back into the room, he brought a drink for Dorothy and ginger ale for Cindy and Gavin.

"Did you pour any for our kids?" Dorothy said.

"They help themselves all the time. They'll do it tonight if they want anything."

Dorothy went out and shouted up the stairs that they could have ginger ale if they wanted any. Ross got up, his glass empty, and went off to mix himself another drink. Jennifer put her head back and closed her eyes for a moment. The chill began to come, the sight of death, the fear. Ever since the call from Ross, the cold fear had been there in her body, behind the other feelings.

Ross came back into the room with Dorothy right behind him.

"He's really putting it away, isn't he?" Dorothy said to Jennifer.

Ross took a long drink without looking at her.

"It's a hard time for all of us," Jennifer said. If they were going to fight, she wanted to leave now. A few more minutes, and she'd take the children back to the motel.

Ross was sitting back in a stuffed chair, his feet over the stool in front of him. He pulled his tie loose. Dorothy sat on a straight chair near the door as if ready to escape. There was a long silence. Jennifer became aware that though she didn't like Dorothy, she counted on her to keep the air alive with a human voice. Left to themselves, Ross and Jennifer would have said nothing at all. Jennifer looked across at her younger brother, moved by the fact that he was the last remaining member of her family, and with a sense both of intimacy and strangeness. Their eyes met.

"You look exhausted," Jennifer said.

"He could have been getting more rest," Dorothy said.

"Sure I could," he said. His speech was beginning to slur a little, and there was an aggressive edge to his voice.

"You could have closed the store for a couple of days."

"I'm closing it tomorrow."

Jennifer couldn't work out what this argument was about.

"We were all brought up to believe that hard work was the basis of all the other virtues," Jennifer said.

"Some families learned other things," Dorothy said.

"Like what?" Jennifer snapped back, not sure what she was reacting to except some sort of veiled insult in Dorothy's words.

"Cindy, would you like some more ginger ale?" Dorothy said.

"No thanks."

"Are you sure? We've got lots."

Cindy shook her head. She hated scenes and knew that she was on the edge of one. Gavin, if this were happening in his own home, would probably have told an outrageous joke, but he was ill at ease here, sat quietly sipping his ginger ale.

Ross had finished another drink. He got up and moved toward the kitchen, stopping to take Jennifer's empty glass out of her hand. Dorothy hadn't finished her drink. He was obviously drunk now. Dorothy's face was tight as she sat on her chair and avoided Jennifer's eyes. After a moment, she got to her feet.

"I'll just give him a hand."

She followed her husband into the kitchen. Their voices were soft at first but growing louder.

"Can we go soon?" Cindy said.

"I'll just have one more drink."

The voices in the kitchen grew louder.

"It's none of your business what I do at the store," Ross said.

Dorothy's voice replied, but it was too quiet to hear. A few more words were exchanged, and there was silence. Ross came back into the room and handed Jennifer a drink, then dropped into his chair. Jennifer sipped the drink, which was lethally strong.

"I can't drink this, Ross. I'd never be able to drive to the motel. I'm going to water it down a little."

"Do as you like," he said.

In the kitchen Dorothy was tidying where there was no mess. She turned to Jennifer as if challenged.

"This drink is too strong for me," Jennifer said. She poured some down the sink and added a lot more ginger ale. Dorothy looked toward her, her eyes angry and sore. Jennifer was afraid that she was about to confide in her. She didn't want the confidence. Whatever was going on, whether Ross was right or wrong, she was on his side, because he was her brother, and because in some kind of way she liked him. She didn't like Dorothy, even now when she seemed hurt and pathetic.

"I'll just drink up and go," Jennifer said. "You must be tired too."

"I've still got the food to make for tomorrow," she said. "For after the funeral."

"Do you want me to come over in the morning and give you a hand?"

"You don't need to bother. The kids will be home from school, and Kim's always a help."

"I'll come over for a while."

Back in the living-room, Jennifer watched her brother's face as he stared straight ahead of him. He was flushed from drinking.

"Are you okay Ross?"

"I'm fine."

Jennifer tried to get rid of her drink quickly. She shouldn't have bothered with it at all. Gavin and Cindy waited stolidly. Jennifer swallowed the liquid. Whatever tension had gone with the first drink had come back with the second. Dorothy was still in the kitchen. Jennifer put down her glass.

"We'd better go now," she said. "It's late."

Ross nodded. As she stood, Gavin and Cindy rose with her. Dorothy met them on the way to the door.

"We'll come over in the morning," Jennifer said.

"We can manage."

"Thanks for the dinner."

"You're very welcome."

They drove into the night. They were all tired and made their way to the motel beds almost without speaking. Jennifer fell asleep quickly, but woke suddenly in the dark knowing that she wouldn't sleep again for hours. It was her form of insomnia. Images, her mother's body in the coffin, Ross slumped in his chair, wound themselves around her. She turned in the bed, unable to get comfortable but trying not to wake Cindy, who was sleeping beside her. In an attempt to comfort herself, she thought of Tom, but she could only think of him in bed with his wife, the woman reaching out to touch him.

Jennifer climbed carefully from the bed and made her way to the small bathroom. She must get back to sleep. She'd be too tired to drive home. They'd have an accident, and the children would be killed. She drank a glass of cold water and looked at her face in the mirror. It was strange and haggard. Some old whore. Tom's whore. He was in bed with his wife. She turned out the light and made her way back to bed. Didn't sleep.

It was beginning to get light when she finally fell asleep. She was lying flat on her back, rigid, to keep from turning and fidgeting any more. She woke in daylight as Cindy climbed out of bed and went toward the bathroom. Jennifer turned her face into the pillow. She heard the sound of the shower. She knew that she wouldn't go back to sleep, but she kept her face in the darkness of the pillow until Cindy came back into the room. Then she sat up.

"Can we leave right after the funeral?" Cindy said.

"We'll go back to the house for a little while and leave from there."

Gavin turned over in bed.

"How'd you sleep?" Jennifer said.

"I dreamed I saw Joe Hill last night," he sang in a western twang.

"Oh shut up," Cindy said.

Gavin made an unpleasant noise with his tongue and lay down on his stomach.

"Who's next in the bathroom?" Jennifer said.

"Go ahead," Gavin said. "I'm going back to sleep."

For breakfast, they drove into town and went to Bestward's, the main-street restaurant where Jennifer remembered gathering with her friends sometimes after classes at the high school. Though it looked the same from outside, the inside was completely changed. She looked around the restaurant for familiar faces, but there were none.

They ate and returned to the motel. They wouldn't dress for the funeral until after they'd gone to Dorothy's. It would give them a reason to leave if one was needed.

When they arrived at the house, Ross had vanished somewhere, and Dorothy and Kim were in the kitchen piling up trays of sandwiches.

"Ted's driving out to the home to get Uncle Ernie," Dorothy said.

"How is he?" Jennifer said. She hadn't seen her mother's elder brother for years.

"He's pretty frail. His hearing isn't too good."

"What about Frank?"

"They're driving up from Toronto this morning. I guess you've likely seen Uncle Frank since I have."

"I saw him a couple of times when we were in Toronto."

Frank was only a year or so older than her mother, both of them much younger than Ernie. Frank had begun as a salesman for a meat-packing company, but at his retirement he was sales manager there. He and his wife Evelyn were pleasant quiet people who'd invited Jennifer and Robert for dinner once or twice when they were living in Toronto.

Frank had seemed to have no life outside his job, and Jennifer wondered what he found to do in retirement.

As Jennifer helped make the sandwiches, Dorothy took cookies from the oven and got out plates and cups. She had two tea-pots and two coffee-pots ready, and in a few minutes Julie arrived back from a nearby store with a selection of soft drinks for the children.

"Will many people be coming back after the funeral?"

"Just family and close friends, but when you count all the children it mounts up."

"It's good of you to go to all this trouble."

"It's only what's right."

Jennifer wondered where Ross was, but she didn't want to ask. In a few minutes he came in with a couple of bottles of liquor and put them down on the kitchen counter.

"That took a while," Dorothy said.

Ross didn't answer, just left the room. Jennifer heard water running in the bathtub upstairs.

When the food was ready, they went to the motel, packed and dressed, checked out. She looked at Gavin and Cindy beside her in their good clothes, the only people in this town she really knew, who recognized her for what she was now, not as a name or face out of the past. Yet they seemed separate from her too. They were other people, almost strangers. No-one knew her.

It was too soon to go to the church so they drove around town, and Jennifer told them stories about the town as she remembered it. In the stories, it was innocent, strange and comic. They were laughing on the way to her mother's funeral. Laughter, tears, a scream of rage; all seemed equally close to her.

They reached the church just as her cousin Ted arrived with his father. Ted's hair was grey now, and his lean body looked awkward in his suit. He was a mechanic, working mostly on trucks and farm machinery, and his hands were scarred and had grease worked into the lines.

Ted was trying to get his father out of the car.

"It won't bend that way, goddamn it," the old man said shrilly in the penetrating voice of one who's losing his hearing, and a woman in an old fur coat stopped on her way up the path to the church and looked toward the car. Ted saw her, and his face reddened. He turned back to his father, took the cane out of his hands and all but lifted him out of the car.

"What are you doing?" the old man shouted. Ted set him on the pavement and handed him back his cane. Jennifer turned to Gavin, who was trying to keep the grin from his face. She gave him a quick smile, and they started into the church. Ted's son Mike met them at the door and led them to one of the front pews. Jennifer noticed several people in the church she didn't recognize. Why were these strangers at her mother's funeral?

When they took their place in the pew, Gavin's eyes moved to the coffin at the front of the church. She took his hand. They waited as Ted and Irene came up the aisle with Uncle Ernie. Frank and Evelyn walked behind them, Evelyn's face as pale as the string of pearls at her neck. Behind Evelyn came Dorothy and her children. For a moment Jennifer didn't recognize the plain-looking man and woman with Dorothy. It was her cousin Phyllis. The man must be her husband.

As Jennifer moved over to make room, she noticed Attler Woodie slip quietly into a back corner of the church.

The minister came in, a clean, precise young man, and the service began. When they stood to sing a hymn, Jennifer heard a strong pleasant tenor voice somewhere behind her and wondered who it could be.

Time like an ever-rolling stream
bears all its sons away;
They die forgotten as a dream
dies at the opening day.

136

Time carried her back. She was in the workshop with Harold and her father; in the house her mother was with the new baby, and Jennifer seemed to have no place there. A smell of fresh glue, the sound of a rasp, the glue boiling slowly in its pot, the winter afternoon dark outside the window. Time bore all its sons away. All its daughters.

The minister began to speak, and beside her Gavin started to cry. She put her arm around him and held him, and in a moment he was still.

At the end of the service, they made their way slowly out to the car to drive to the cemetery. Jennifer found herself beside Dorothy. As they stood waiting for Uncle Ernie to move ahead of them, Dorothy looked across at the church. She saw someone, and her face changed, the skin drawing into a tight anger. Jennifer wanted to follow her look, but Dorothy could see her.

It was cold outside after the warm church. Under the cover of heavy grey cloud, the coffin was carried to the hearse, and they drove through the familiar streets to the cemetery. On a streetcorner, an unknown man took off his hat as the funeral passed. At the cemetery they walked over wet grass. It was on a hill at the edge of town, and the fields of dark earth and bare trees spread toward the horizon. There was a cold wind, and a few drops of rain fell. Pale cornstalks shook in the wind.

All the members of the family stood round as the body was placed in the earth. The expression on her Uncle Frank's face was almost impassive, but tears rolled down his cheeks. Brother and sister: one of the mysteries. This was her family gathered beside her. These people were her blood and kin. She looked at them to avoid the sight of the grave. Ted and Ross: there was something about their faces that she saw and could hardly bear. The pain of old-fashioned responsible men in their maturity and blindness. The terrible smalltown reticence, the inarticulate blundering goodwill. Harold going dutifully to work at fourteen as if no other life was conceivable. The coffin had vanished. The minister spoke. Jennifer began to cry and felt Cindy take her arm. As they were moving away, she could see Uncle Ernie coming toward her. As a child Jennifer had been frightened of him.

"You look like her, you know," he said. "In the eyes."

"How have you been keeping?"

"I'm not worth a damn. Can't hear. Can't walk right. Not worth a damn."

"You seem pretty spry."

He didn't hear or ignored it.

"When we get to the house, you see that I get a drink, Jenny. Ted won't let me drink. You get me a drink."

"All right," she said. They were almost at the cars. Ted noticed that his father was missing and came to collect him.

"C'mon Dad. The car's down here."

"I can talk to Jenny if I like."

"Talk to her when you get to the house."

The gathering at Ross' house began with a certain solemnity, but now and then it would become lively with chatter and then subside. Jennifer had a couple of sandwiches and one weak drink. Ted looked at her as she took a drink to his father, but he made no move to take it away. Not that he would have dared. Uncle Ernie would have created a row if he did.

"Do we have to stay long?" Cindy said after the first few minutes.

"No. But have something to eat so we don't have to stop on the road."

"I'm not hungry."

"Have a sandwich."

Jennifer herself was starved, felt almost embarrassed by her appetite. She finished her drink and was making her way to the kitchen to fill her glass with water when she heard Dorothy's voice.

"She has a nerve coming to the church."

138

"No reason she shouldn't," Ross said.

"No reason she should."

"It's a gesture of respect."

"She should be old enough to know what's decent."

"I told you before, there's nothing going on between me and her."

"Don't try to tell me that."

"There's no point talking about it now with all these people in the house."

"By the time they leave, you'll likely be too drunk to talk about anything."

"And if I am?"

"You can go to her when you're in that state."

"Maybe I will."

Jennifer turned and moved quietly away, ashamed that she'd stood listening so long but wanting Ross to know she had heard, that she was on his side always. There was no way to say it. She told Cindy and Gavin they were going to leave and began to move around the room saying her good-byes. Uncle Ernie insisted on getting up out of his chair to give her a kiss, and as he was lifting himself, he pushed against Jimmy, Ross's young son and caused him to spill a glass of ginger ale. Dorothy, who was nearby, dealt Jimmy a stinging slap for the spill.

She was near the door of the room when she met Ted.

"I hear you're a grandfather now."

"You should come round and see her."

"I wish we could, but we have to get back. Robert's in the hospital and Cindy's worried about him."

"We had a spell during the winter."

"Your gall-bladder."

He nodded.

"I've been thinking about Harold a lot the last few days. You were close friends, weren't you?"

"I think about him sometimes. You know Irene was interested in him before I ever really knew her. If he hadn't got killed, the two of them might have got married."

"I didn't know that."

"Not many people did. They kept pretty quiet about it. Funny how things happen eh?"

"It's nice to see you again, Ted."

"You don't get back to town much."

"No."

"I suppose you'll be back less than ever now your mother's gone."

"I suppose so."

He sounded regretful and puzzled. Why had she gone away?

It had been inevitable, somehow, from her childhood. Not that she was unhappy here, but it was always a place she liked but wouldn't stay. In a way, leaving town was the one creative act of her life, the one decision that led inevitably to all the others. Some vision of a wider world had led her on, but she couldn't say to what, only that she and Ted were different. But perhaps they always had been, the future inevitable in the chemistry of their cells.

She shook hands with Ted and rounded up the children. Ross and Dorothy met them at the door.

"Thanks," Jennifer said, "for everything. An awful lot of the work's fallen on you."

"You must come back for a real visit sometime," Dorothy said.

"We'll try."

"I'll let you know about the estate," Ross said. "I'm afraid she didn't leave a will."

"Let me know. I'll come up if it's necessary."

"Are you sure you wouldn't like to stay the night and start off bright and early in the morning?" Dorothy said.

"No. We'd better go."

She looked at Ross, tried to reach his eyes, but he didn't look at her. She stretched out her hand to him.

"Take care of yourself Ross. Thanks again Dorothy.

You've been marvellous."

They made their way to the car. As they drove down the street, they passed a boy on a bicycle.

"Why can't elephants ride bicycles?" Gavin said.

"I don't know."

"They don't have any thumb to ring the little bell."

"You've told that one before," Cindy said.

"You two were very good the last two days. These things aren't easy."

Neither of the children spoke. She pulled the car onto the highway to Toronto. She had driven down this road on a bus to start university. Had driven down it with Robert after their wedding. Leaving home for the last time. To the years in London and then back in Toronto.

They'd been comfortable in England, but after a few years Robert had begun to feel some sense of exile. When they left Canada, there had been some unspoken assumption that in the rich milieu of Europe there must be some kind of creative blossoming for him, but it hadn't happened. When they came back to Canada for his mother's funeral, they'd felt lost. The country had changed while they were away, and they were no part of the change.

While they were in Toronto on that trip, Robert had talked to people in a few publishing houses, and when they returned to London, had begun a correspondence that led to the offer of a job. They were frightened to return, deeply dependent on their London habits and acquaintances, Jennifer especially. Canada had grown less interesting to her in their time away from it. She hadn't felt the need to escape that Robert had, but once settled in England, she felt no need to return. But she agreed to come back for a while and try it.

The next four years spelt the final end of their marriage. It had been born in Toronto, and it died there. They arrived back in 1964. The Vietnam war was flourishing; politics was drunk like water. They rented a house in the Annex and before long began to take in draft-dodgers and deserters.

It began with such exhilaration. Robert had always felt the compulsion to give himself to something, and hypersensitive as he always was to the deadness of the respectable civic world, the world his parents had inhabited, he'd taken from Marx a vocabulary that replaced duty with history, but that only left him a prisoner of abstraction, for his vocabulary had little to do with his real experience. His words and his life had found no place to meet. But now it was different. They were part of a group, a dozen groups. The complex issues of their CND days fell away as they huddled on the border of a nation that was expending its children in an insane, unjust, unwinnable war.

Before they left Canada, the United States had been taken for granted in a way that made it omnipotent but almost invisible. In England, they'd been part of the theoretical anti-Americanism of the British left, and this had prepared them for the seductive grandeur of hating the Vietnam war.

They began working on the committees that were helping draft evaders. Then a boy named Hugh came to live in a room in their basement. He was a quiet polite good-natured boy. The terrible paradigm: some madman wanted to send this kindly boy to be killed in a foreign jungle in defence of an indefensible regime. They fed Hugh and became his friends. He helped look after the children. Cindy was in Grade One and Gavin was still at home. Each day Hugh would take him to a park near the house while Jennifer did her cleaning. Hugh was their friend, a pleasant young companion, but his presence also gave them a sense of rightness. They were part of a cause.

Hugh found a job and left. He was replaced by someone else. And someone else. The war went on. The issues multiplied. As she thought about it now, she saw a skeletal image of the house with a strange energy rising out of that basement room. Music. Drugs. They learned to take marijuana

142

for granted. They listened to Bob Dylan. One or two of the young men who lived in the basement room were burning with righteous anger. One was clearly mad, and yet at the time Jennifer couldn't bring herself to say those words: Phillip is crazy, he should be put away. He was a refugee from madness, therefore he must be sane. But she wouldn't leave him alone in the house with the children.

When he left to join in the destruction of Rochdale, his room stank. He had pissed on the floor. In a drawer were a few unidentified white pills that Jennifer flushed down the toilet. When the police came looking for him, she protected him, though she knew where he could be found. His girl-friend came to see them, covered with bruises, and they tried to comfort her. They accepted all this, almost desired it.

Somewhere around that time she'd read an article called "On the Necessity of Violation." At parties, women in mini-skirts arched their backs and bent their legs in rhythm with the snarling rage of "Like a Rolling Stone."

The issues multiplied. For the first time, there was talk of "branch plants," and Robert found himself on the wrong side, working for one. They drank more than they ever had in England. They smoked pot, and Robert hallucinated for hours. But the greatest intoxicant was a single word. Freedom. Freedom Rider. Freedom Fighter. They were stoned on apocalypse. They talked of taking the children out of school. They were on the board of a group gathered to found a free school.

Through all this, their bodies came together like iron hammers. Naked bodies were the banners of this new cru-sade. They demanded some ecstasy of pain and honesty and flesh and never achieved it. They'd grown used to the men who lived in the basement bringing their women with them. It was the usual pattern to have two couples in the house, and they even made some attempt to make decisions demo-cratically.

Robert became more uneasy about his position in a branch-plant publishing company. Suddenly, to be a Canadian was a call to arms. He talked of leaving and starting a new publishing house, but at the same time he was compelled as never before to work splendidly for his American masters. As his politics became more idealistic, he became more concerned that his books should make money.

The last of those to live in the basement was Eddie Chaplett. He was a deserter, bright, silent, secretive. At first he kept apart from them, but gradually he became part of the house. A girl named Lisa moved in with him. She was a small girl with a shapely body about which she seemed to have no sense of privacy or shame. She was a symptom of the new world, usually half naked, always a little stoned. The four of them would meet to talk over questions of running the house. Sometimes the children were included in the meetings. Now and then, late at night, Eddie would talk about himself. He was a poor boy who'd joined the army to escape and found it a rapid education. He'd deserted from an army camp in Texas, and as he told the story, his trip to the Canadian border had been harrowing, with episodes in smalltown jails and encounters with every freak the American highways could produce. He told his stories in a flat, humourless, insistent voice. Other times he'd be silent for days.

The four of them began to spend more and more time together. They became a unit at parties. Robert and Lisa danced. Jennifer and Eddie watched, occasionally talked. Robert wanted Lisa; they all saw that. Jennifer said nothing. When Robert was openly affectionate with Lisa, Jennifer burned. She felt stiff and tight that she couldn't be like this girl. She tried to be accepting. He'd had other women before, but she hadn't known them, hadn't been forced to watch. Eddie was unreadable as he moved around them, watching. Sometimes Jennifer thought he wanted her; at others he seemed to dislike her.

144

One night Robert and Lisa vanished from a party. Jennifer couldn't smile and let them be. The cold panic of jealousy that she'd held restrained burst its bonds. She rushed around the strange house, opening doors, looking for them. They were gone. Her body shook with chills. Eddie followed quietly after her as she walked out and started to run down the street. Their house wasn't far away; she ran all the way there and into the house. The bedroom door was closed, but they were there. She stood by the door hearing them, unable to draw herself away. She was sick with jealousy; she wanted to open the door. At the end of the hall, Eddie was watching her. She moved away from the bedroom door, each step a terrible effort ending in a fall through space.

She followed Eddie to the room in the basement. It was inevitable. Everything was pushing her toward him. As she walked behind him he seemed a complete stranger. She was still listening for sounds from upstairs.

Beside the bed, Eddie was taking off his clothes and putting them on a chair. His eyes were on her. She shivered as she began to undress. She was frightened. She'd only had two men in her life, Robert and Colin. Still, she wanted to be held, she wanted comfort. She told herself she must be open to what was offered. She took off her brassière, self-conscious about the fall of her big breasts. Lisa was so small and young. She slid her fingers under the elastic of her underpants, took them off. Eddie stood by the bed, waiting for her, his cock erect. As she climbed on the bed, he didn't touch her. She lay down on her side and waited for him to take her in his arms. The bed dipped as he climbed on. He knelt on the mattress, turned her over on her front and lifted her hips toward him. It was cold and brutal. He didn't kiss or fondle her, just put her in place and shoved his cock in as far as he could. She shook with terror as he fucked her, holding her by the bones of the pelvis and jamming her against him harder and harder until it hurt her. There was no sound except the repeated collision. Then he stiffened and held her tight against him, still silent as the sperm poured out.

He withdrew and lay down, his face away from her. Jennifer bit her arm to keep from crying out. She lay still till he seemed asleep, then made her way upstairs and lay down on a couch. During the night, she heard Lisa go down the stairs to the basement. She held her breath so the girl wouldn't notice her. She lay awake all night. In the morning, she got up before the children and kept herself busy in the kitchen. She cleaned out and scrubbed all the cupboards, cleaned behind the stove and fridge. She gave Cindy and Gavin their breakfast and began to scrub the floor.

When Robert came down, she didn't speak or look at him. She couldn't. He made himself coffee.

"Tonight the four of us should talk things over," he said quietly. He sounded frightened.

"I won't be here."

She hadn't known the words were going to come out. She plunged the rag in the hot soapy water and rinsed a patch of floor.

"Why not?"

"I can't stand it."

"It's a chance to liberate ourselves."

Jennifer looked up for the first time, looked at his face, the look of serious concern. She hated him.

"Do you want to know what he did to me?" She wouldn't let herself cry. She hung on, hard, hard.

He was silent. She held him with her eyes.

"Shall we have a group discussion about whether I want to be fucked like a dog? A dog . . . shit . . . a dog would have showed more kindness . . . I'm going away. I'm finished."

She stood up, sobbing, tripped on the bucket, spilling soapy water all over the floor, and walked out of the house. It was a cold day; her feet were wet and she had no coat, but she walked for an hour like that, hardly feeling the chill.

She could never tell anyone about that night. Maybe Tom, someday. But who was he, that she could expose her humiliation to him? What if he decided to stay with his wife? It was a family; they belonged together, as she belonged with Robert.

No. Her marriage to Robert was over that morning in Toronto. She knew it even then. Though she would go back, and they'd try again and move to Kingston and try again, it was over. She didn't love him. All the attempts were doomed; blind, deaf, dwarfed gestures that had no hope of life.

Robert, solitude, Tom, some hypothetical future man: the choice was really simpler than that. It was Tom or being alone.

It was Tom. She would pay the price. She drove on into the darkening afternoon.

"Will I be home in time to see Daddy?" Cindy said.

Jennifer looked at her watch.

"Probably just make it."

"Good."

When they reached Kingston, she dropped Cindy and Gavin at the hospital and drove herself home. By the time they got back from the hospital, she'd walked mechanically through the steps of preparing a simple supper, but even with all three of them there, it seemed to her that they couldn't fill the emptiness of the house. They were like tiny figures in some huge building that dwarfed and isolated them. Jennifer waited for Tom to phone, but no call came. She wished there was someplace she could call him.

She'd just got home from work the next afternoon when the phone rang. She picked it up expecting to hear Tom's voice, but it was Barbara.

"Are we still going to that concert, Jenny?"

"I'd forgotten all about it."

"It's at 8.30."

"I don't know if I'm up to it."

And she wanted to be home in case Tom phoned.

"You should come, it'll do you good to get out."

Perhaps it was silly to wait for his call. He'd phone when he could. Barbara asked about the funeral, and Jennifer talked about it, but it remained at a distance. By the end of the conversation, she'd decided to go to the concert. It would be over early. Maybe to go somewhere with Barbara would ease her guilt.

Barbara was late coming to pick her up, and by the time they got to the hall most of the seats were filled. They took places near the back, and Jennifer glanced over the program notes in the few minutes before the lights went down. It was a concert of English songs by a man who taught at the university.

He seemed to Jennifer a mediocre singer though there was an expressive quality that was sometimes convincing. Still, she remained at a distance from it all until the last song before the intermission. It was a folk song found in Newfoundland but English in form. He sang it unaccompanied, and while the vocal quality was no better, there was a kind of passionate conviction in the performance that moved her.

She's like the swallow that flies so high,
She's like the river that never runs dry,
She's like the sunshine on the lee shore,
She loves her love, but she'll love no more.

It was one of those familiar ballads of love and betrayal with a pretty plaintive tune. One way or another, Jennifer thought, everyone was surrounded by lost loves.

At the end of the song, the singer left the stage and the lights went on. Jennifer turned toward the aisle and saw Tom walking past. With a woman. His wife. Barbara was looking the other way and hadn't noticed them. His wife

148

was a slender, pretty woman, a little like Barbara in style. At the sight of the two of them, Jennifer began to shake. She turned her head and saw them go into the lobby. If she and Barbara went out there, Barbara would see them.

"I think I'd like to go now," she said to Barbara. "You stay if you like."

"No, I'll come. I'm not enjoying it much."

They picked up their coats and walked toward the door. Jennifer tried to lead Barbara away from the direction in which she'd seen Tom go, but as they were crossing the lobby, Barbara suddenly took her arm.

"Oh Jenny," she said.

Jennifer didn't look, just made her way to the door. The first thing was to get out, to get away.

"Did you see him?" Barbara said when they were outside.

Jennifer said nothing. She didn't want to pretend.

"Tom was there with his wife. I'm glad we were on our way out."

Jennifer walked ahead through the cold air. This is unbearable, she was saying to herself, and at the same time keeping her face a blank, trying to walk normally.

"I suppose I'll have to get used to this kind of thing happening. I'm sure to meet them sooner or later."

Jennifer was furious with her for talking, for sounding childish. Why wouldn't she shut up? It wasn't necessary to babble. But it wasn't fair to blame Barbara for not knowing what she felt, not recognizing that Jennifer had betrayed her.

"I'm glad I was with you when it happened, Jenny. It helps to be with someone who knows. Think what it would be like if I was with Al. I guess the first time is the worst. I know her a little bit from the nursery-school. I'll even have to talk to her eventually."

"What's she like?" Jennifer said.

She couldn't resist the question, though it might make Barbara suspicious. But why would it? She had no idea, would never have dreamed that Jennifer was involved with Tom.

"She seems nice. A bit stand-offish, I guess. She's pretty, isn't she?"

"Yes."

She'd only got a momentary glimpse of the woman, like something seen by the flash of a strobe light. A photograph blurred by movement. She tried to remember details about her. If they met, would she sense that Jennifer was her husband's mistress?

"It's things like this that make me feel like such a kid," Barbara was saying. "Why can't I deal with anything?"

"I don't know if anyone can really."

They reached the corner where her path and Barbara's would separate. She should invite her in for coffee or a drink, but she wanted to be left alone.

"Do you want to come to my place and have coffee?" she said.

"No. You must be worn out after the funeral and everything. I'll just go home. I think I'm over the worst of it now."

Jennifer didn't insist. They parted, and she turned toward home. There was just that moment, a man and a woman seen and then gone.

She tidied the house and went to bed though it was still early. Loneliness was like a vacuum around her, sucking out her breath. She could get back out of bed, but there was nothing to do, nothing to be done. As well to lie still, breathing slowly in and out, her arms wrapped tightly round her.

But sleep didn't come, and she lay there in a kind of waking dream of the moment when the man and woman moved past her. Other men and women: Barbara and Al, her mother and father, Ross and Dorothy, men and women in pairs, Robert and Jennifer. They moved past and were gone. She tried to see herself and Tom as one of the couples, but she couldn't. No effort of will allowed her to see them together. It was always Tom and his wife, her trying to pull them apart, the woman turning to her, her look making everything whirl in giddy confusion. The look of the moment when she realized what Jennifer was trying to do, the pain, and then the body became a figure of flame, and the figure had her mother's face.

6

Jennifer looked out the window at the snow swirling across the December darkness. If she had decent shoes on, it might have been fun to walk home, but when she came out in the morning she had given no thought to the predicted storm and had put on a pair of low shoes that would be soaked in the first few feet. The door of the staff-room opened, and she turned to see Irving come in.

"I've got good news," he said. "I've been trying to get to see you all day."

"Personal or professional good news?"

"Both."

"Which do I get first?"

"Personal. They've finally found out what's wrong with Deborah."

"And it's not serious?"

"Serious enough, but they can cure it. Some obscure and persistent intestinal infection. It needs a combination of drugs and a special diet, but she should be well in a month."

"You've been looking so worried I didn't dare ask about her."

"I was so scared I could hardly function. I've been doing a lousy job around here. As you've probably noticed."

"So why do you have good news professionally?"

"McAdam."

"What's he been up to."

"Doing what I should have been doing. He's got a place for Melinda at the Centre for Crippled Children. It'll get her out of her, and the Centre will work with the Children's Aid to try and get her some kind of foster home."

"That's great," Jennifer said, and yet she felt uneasy. Why did it have to be McAdam? It was stupid to think that. It didn't matter how the job was done as long as it was done. She gave Irving a hug.

"Now we've only got three more."

"It's a long way to the fair for those three."

"Don't discourage me in the midst of success."

"You want a ride home?"

"Yes. I wore the wrong shoes. I'd be soaked even waiting for the bus."

Irving pointed out his car at the edge of the lot.

"I'll be out in five minutes. The door's open."

He walked out of the room. Jennifer looked back out at the snow, wondering if it would continue overnight. Tomorrow she was going to Toronto to meet Tom, who was there on some kind of business, and she didn't want anything to stop her. It was a treat she had promised herself, to be alone with him someplace where they didn't have to be discreet. Jennifer was tired of being careful.

She put on her coat and set out for Irving's car. A couple of inches of snow had fallen already, and the ground was slippery underfoot as she walked. When she reached the car, Irving wasn't there, but as she settled in the front seat, she saw a dark figure moving toward her through the swirling white fragments. He walked quickly, his head down. Jennifer would have liked to tell him about Tom, almost resolved to, then changed her mind.

How long was it going to be a secret? It was out of her hands, and she wouldn't ask Tom. He would talk about the future when he was ready, and until then Jennifer would keep silent.

The roads hadn't been plowed or sanded, and Irving, not much of a driver at the best of times, seemed about to kill them several times.

"These conditions are terrible."

Jennifer agreed silently and hung onto the edge of the seat.

"I can't keep it from skidding."

Again the car slipped sideways.

Somehow they reached her house in one piece, but when he tried to pull away, the wheels began to spin. Jennifer went to the back of the car and pushed as the back tires spun. At last they grabbed, throwing snow all over her feet and ankles. She waved at the car as it vanished into the blizzard. Irving didn't look back.

As Jennifer was walking up the steps of the porch, she slipped and fell, landing heavily on her left hip. Pain made her wince as she climbed back up.

"Damn it all to hell," she said aloud.

Cold, wet and angry, she made her way into the house. Cindy was sitting at the kitchen table doing her homework. She might have done something about supper.

"I just fell on the porch, and I'm soaking wet," Jennifer said. "I'm damned if I'm going to cook. Why don't you order some pizza?"

"I already did. Gavin and I didn't think you'd want to cook after getting home in this."

"I got a ride with Irving, but he kept trying to kill us. I'm going to change."

Jennifer came back down in her dressing-gown and opened a beer.

"You should have hot toddy on a night like this," Cindy said.

"This will do."

She had no sooner sat down with the beer than the phone rang. It was a strange voice.

"Mrs. Mallen, please."

"Speaking."

"My name's Mary Slyfield. I'm Eugene's mother. You remember my son? Eugene?"

"Yes."

"I was down to visit him yesterday. He says he wants to see you."

"Why?"

"For a visit. He said not one of his friends from Kingston has been to see him." She paused for a response; not receiving one, she went on. "He's hoping you'll come. I said I'd phone you."

"He's in Napanee, isn't he?"

"The Quinte Regional Detention Centre."

"I don't have a car. I don't know if I'd be able to get there."

"He mentioned you particularly as someone he wanted to see."

"Is it about the preliminary hearing?"

"I don't know about any of that. That's in the hands of the lawyers. I just know that there's a lonely boy there who'd like to see you."

To get what you want, be unfair.

"I'll do my best to get to see him," Jennifer said.

Someone was knocking at the door. It must be the pizza.

"I'm sorry. I have to go now. There's someone at the door."

"I know he'll be pleased to see you."

Jennifer hung up the phone. Cindy had answered the door and was looking for money. Between the two of them, they found it, paid the man who had made the delivery and got out the plates.

"Was that about Eugene?" Cindy said.

"Yes. His mother wants me to go and visit him."

"Are you going to?"

"Probably."

"I wouldn't."

"Why?"

"Because he's creepy."

"Creepy people get lonely too."

Gavin came into the room to hear the last of this.

"They should start a Lonely Creeps Club."

The exchange with Cindy decided Jennifer. She must go and see Eugene. For all the reasons she didn't want to. He needed someone to pay some attention to him if he was to have any hope of living a real life. It would be so easy to turn her face from him now. He had elected Jennifer as his friend; she must accept that election.

"You two all set for the weekend?" she said.

"Daddy's coming to pick us up at ten."

"How is he?"

"He says he's okay now."

"I hope so."

"Do you really?" Cindy said.

"Of course. Do you think I wish him evil just because we can't live together?"

"Your voice always sounds funny when you talk to him. As if you were mad."

"He gets pretty angry with me too."

"I think he'd like to come back."

"And it would be fine for a week or two. Then we'd start to make each other miserable again."

"I don't know why."

"You may not believe this, Cindy, but neither do I. I can't explain it in any words that make sense, but when we're together, something bad happens to both of us."

"I don't think Daddy feels that way."

"When he's sick and lonely, of course the idea of being with us is appealing, but it wouldn't satisfy him."

"I think it would."

"Well, it's not going to happen," Jennifer said. The food that she was chewing seemed tasteless, heavy. She chewed mechanically.

155

When they had finished eating, and the children had left the table, Jennifer sat and finished her beer before cleaning up. She thought about clothes for the trip, tried to imagine what Tom might like. It was foolish to try to dress for him. It was for the young to do that, each a new mirror to the other, in love with their reflection in the lover's eyes. Tom wouldn't care how she dressed. Or would he? It frightened her that she didn't know.

When she had tidied the kitchen, she went to the basement and did a couple of loads of washing. While they were in the machine, she ironed a pile of shirts and blouses. For a while Gavin worked at the old desk in the corner, then he turned on the television set to watch *M.A.S.H.* and *All in the Family*. Jennifer kept half an eye on the set as she worked. Cindy came down with a tin of Coke and stared into the grey shapes.

Jennifer liked ironing, producing that smooth perfection. Now and then housework gave her the satisfying feeling that she was putting the world in order. But within a few hours, the order would vanish and her satisfaction with it.

Gavin was reading a comic-book while he watched television. She could never understand how he did it. It must be bad for him; he would never learn to concentrate. She unplugged the iron and carried upstairs the clothes she had done. Outside the streets were silent with snow.

She had packed her clothes for Toronto and settled the kids for the night when she heard a noise. Footsteps on the porch. How could anyone appear out of that white silence? A knock. She went to answer.

It was Barbara, who met Jennifer's eyes for a moment and then looked deliberately away. She didn't speak, only brushed the snow off her shoulders and hair before coming into the hall and taking off her boots on the carpet. There was something wrong. Jennifer didn't want to know what.

"The snow's getting deep," she said.

"Yes."

Barbara left her things in the hall and walked into the living-room. She turned abruptly.

"Al saw you with Tom. He thinks you're having an affair. Not that he knows it means anything to me. He told me as if it was some kind of dirty joke." She turned to look at Jennifer for a long moment, held her with those pale blue eyes. Jennifer felt a dry sickness move down her throat. She had said she would pay the price.

"Is it true?"

She gathered her courage.

"Yes."

"How could you do that to me Jenny?"

"I couldn't help it," she said. It was feeble, flat. She turned away so that Barbara couldn't see her face. She wanted not to be here, but there was no way out.

"I don't know what you mean, that you couldn't help it. Two months ago you didn't even know him. You must have gone out of your way to see him. You must have wanted to do it."

"He was the judge at the preliminary hearing where I had to testify."

"That hardly counts as being thrown together by fate. It's not exactly like being shipwrecked on a desert island."

"I don't know what I can say."

"You must have set out to humiliate me."

"No."

"That's how it looks to me."

"That's not how it was."

"You knew that I'd tried to kill myself, and you just went right ahead."

"I guess I did. I had a bad time at the hearing, and he took me to lunch. Something happened."

"He sure seizes every opportunity. I wonder how many other women he has on his string."

Jennifer couldn't speak. There were no others. Barbara had no right to say that. But how did she know for sure?

157

Did she know him at all? Right now she knew no-one, least of all herself. Something was tightening, hardening in her. Anger.

"God I can't stand this," Barbara said.

"I didn't want to hurt you."

Jennifer wasn't sure if that was true. There was something about Barbara that had always roused her anger and contempt.

"Have you . . . slept with him?"

"Yes."

"Jesus Christ." She brought her small hand down hard on a table and rocked the lamp that sat there. "Why does he sleep with you and not with me? Do I smell or something?"

Jennifer wanted to walk out of the house. She had to escape from this woman's voice.

"Is he good in bed? Don't tell me, I don't want to know . . . but I do. I want to know everything. I can't bear this, Jenny. Why did it have to happen? I wasn't happy before, but I was used to it. Now nothing's worthwhile. I don't want to live like this."

Then don't, Jennifer said in her mind, but out loud she said: "It'll get better."

"No. I don't think it will. Maybe I'll get anaesthetized again so I can walk around like a windup toy, but it's never going to get better. He was everything I wanted, and I can't have him. He didn't want me enough to risk anything. I was just a pleasant companion, pretty in a superficial way. Shallow, that's it, isn't it? I'm shallow. There isn't much to me. Al's been bored for years."

Jennifer felt more and more that she was trapped by the terrible insistent voice. Why wouldn't Barbara go away? She had to be rid of her.

"I should have more dignity. I hate you for what you've done to me, but here I am telling you . . ."

Barbara sat heavily on the couch. She started to cry and

buried her face in a cushion. She was asking for comfort, but Jennifer had none to give. She felt no affection, only guilt and anger. Barbara looked foolish, her body strained and ugly. The tears subsided, and she looked up.

"Is he going to leave his wife or are you satisfied to be his mistress?" It was cheap and sneering.

Jennifer stiffened.

"I don't know. I can't say."

"You're managing to forget she's there. The way you forgot I was there."

Jennifer made herself iron, forced the words out of her mind. The anger in her was ready to break out. Barbara stood up from the couch, went and looked out the window at the flickering snow. When she turned back to Jennifer, her body seemed dry and contorted. Jennifer had never seen anything so ugly.

"I don't think we can be friends any more, Jenny."

So smug in the easy role of suffering victim.

"I don't know what makes you think we ever were friends," Jennifer said. She felt a terrible sense of angry triumph.

The pale eyes were wide with shock and distress. Now she'd go away. The voice would stop.

"You're my best friend," it said weakly.

Jennifer met the pale eyes, held them with her own. She didn't speak. There was no need. Barbara turned away and started to walk out of the room. She stumbled near the door but caught hold of the wall to right herself, took up her coat and boots and left the house. When the door closed, Jennifer collapsed in a chair with her face in her hands. There was a sharp pain in her head. Everything seemed to be flying away, getting bigger as she shrank to nothing. She tried to control her breathing. Stood up and made her way blindly to the kitchen and found a glass to get some water, but she was too unsteady, and when she put the glass on the counter, her hand wouldn't open to let go. It was tight inside her clenched fist, and her fingers closed their grip on the glass until it broke.

She looked down toward her hand. Somehow it wasn't cut, and she left the pieces of glass on the counter and ran up the stairs to Gavin's room. He was on the edge of sleep, spoke in a blurred voice as she bent over him and held him and kissed his face. She hugged him tight in her arms for a long time. Then she went slowly downstairs and opened a bottle of beer. She sat still in a chair, drinking one beer after another until she began to feel she might be able to sleep.

Before she went up to bed, she walked to the front door and stared at the magic movement of the snow. She opened the door and walked out, barefoot, stood there perfectly still, as if waiting for something to come, some message, some messenger. Sharp pains began in her feet from the cold snow and then began to shoot up her legs. She returned to the house and locked the door behind her.

Once in bed, she fell asleep quickly, but she woke later in the darkness, shaken by a dream. She had been standing by the side of some body of water, it seemed like a deep pool, the water a curious opaque grey. Cindy was in the pool. At first she seemed to be standing on something with just her head revealed, but then she began to sink and struggle while Jennifer stood paralyzed, unable to move and save her. As she tried to come closer, she seemed to go further away. She noticed that Tom was on the other side of the pool, smiling, with a group of men in strange costumes from some other century. Then Jennifer was on that side of the pool, but she was invisible. Cindy was going under the water, only her hands were visible, and for a long time the two hands waved, mimed her drowning. Just as they were about to disappear, Tom reached out and took hold of one of her hands and drew her out of the water. As she came out of the water, Cindy was naked and smiling. Tom reached out and began to play with her breasts. Once again, Jennifer tried to cry out, but she was invisible and drifting away. It was then she woke.

Her body felt hot and stiff. She threw off the covers. The images of the dream suffocated her. They seemed connected with the ache in her legs and back. Her mouth was dry.

She threw back the covers and climbed out of bed. Made her way through the dark to the bathroom. She drank a glass of water, then turned the light off and stood looking out the window across the backyard. The branches of the trees were covered with snow. The full moon cast shadows. There was a light in the house behind. Mr. Parkman, who lived there, was a retired postman. She wondered if he was always up at this hour.

Jennifer went back to bed, but sleep wouldn't come. As she moved around the bed in an attempt to get comfortable, she grew frightened: the terror that this emptiness would last forever. She tried to tell herself that it was only the hour and her sleeplessness that produced the anxiety, but without success. She remembered the look on Barbara's face.

At last she slept, to wake in the morning feeling stale and unrested, but after coffee and food she felt a little better and got the children up and organized for Robert's arrival. He drove up in front, honked the horn, and they went to him, leaving her the silence and solitude of the house, a moment's sheer rest. She went up to the bathroom and started the tub. She bathed, shaved her legs, put lotion on her skin and dusted herself with a sweet-smelling powder. After the train trip she would be stale enough, smelling of the train, of other people's cigarettes, but at least she would start clean. If only she could be clean inside.

She slept on the train, perhaps making up a little for the sleepless night. She woke near Port Hope with a stiff neck. There was no snow here, and the land was dark and bare as the train made its way into the endless suburbs of Toronto. Under the immensely high arched roof of Union Station, Tom was waiting for her. He put his arms around her. A black ticket-clerk looked toward them as if they were familiar to him.

"Barbara came to see me last night," she said as they walked out to the street. "She knows."

"How?"

"Al saw us together."

"It must have been hard for you."

She wanted to tell him about it, but it wasn't possible. Not yet. He put an arm around her and hugged her as he waved with his other hand for a taxi.

"You're very clever," she said.

"Why?"

"You can hug me and wave for a taxi at the same time."

He laughed and opened the cab door for her. He kept his arm around her on the ride up to Bloor. As they walked into the hotel, she turned to him.

"Did you say your wife was meeting you?"

"No. A friend."

"How honest of you."

"I told you I'm like that."

When they reached the room, Tom put down her bags and turned to hold her. She reached up toward him, and they kissed.

"I must smell of the train."

"Just your clothes."

"I'll take them off."

They began to undress. Tom, as always, put his clothes down carefully so they didn't crease, his glasses in the pocket of his shirt. It made her smile. When she was naked, he noticed the bruise on her hip.

"What's that?"

"I fell on the porch stairs last night."

He knelt beside her and kissed the bruise.

"It looks like a map," he said, "of a new planet."

His hands stroked her, fingers moved into the hair between her thighs. He kissed the bruise again, then lifted her and carried her to the bed. As he lay down beside her, she reached out her arms and held him tight, rolled over to pull him down on top of her. He lifted his hips and entered her. He was slow, almost impassive; solid and warm. She breathed deeply, and her body shivered into a sudden orgasm that was like a breath of light on water. The light contractions feathered away into the warmth of their motion. She put her hands on his back and felt the movement of muscles under his skin. He held her more tightly, and his breathing grew louder.

When it was over, they lay together, quiet, sated. Gradually they drew a little apart but always with some part of their bodies touching, as if not to break the magic circle. Tom ran his fingers down her back. Jennifer put her head on Tom's chest, her cheek against the thick curly hair. She rubbed his stomach.

"Muscles," she said quietly.

"All the swimming."

"The judge is all wet."

"I saw something nice yesterday afternoon," Tom said. "A bus-driver stopped his bus at an intersection, got out and helped a girl in a wheelchair over two curbs, then went back to his bus."

"Toronto the Good."

"You can judge the level of civilization of any city by its public-transit employees."

"That's a new theory."

"Not a bad one."

"Have you ever lived in England?"

"No."

"The bus-conductors are lovely. At least they used to be. From what I read in the newspapers, England seems to be drowning in bitterness now, but it used to be fun to watch the conductors in action. The good ones were at least half entertainer. But if you got on the subway, people were like zombies, staring straight ahead, hiding behind newspapers."

"Subways must produce different kinds of crime too."

Jennifer rolled over on top of him, pressed her breasts against him and kissed his mouth. He hugged her tightly.

"Who would have expected this?" she said. "That day in court."

"As it happens, I would."

"Why?"

"You seemed so brave on the stand, and a bit naive. I suddenly realized what an attractive woman you are."

"How was I naive?"

"Trying to protect that little weasel."

"Eugene?"

"Yes."

"That's a hard thing for a judge to say."

"I'm not in court."

"Eugene's sick."

"Sick isn't an adequate word for that kind of behaviour. It's an evasion."

"You sound like a hanging judge," Jennifer said. She drew a little away, surprised at what she was hearing him say. She felt for a chill moment that she didn't know him.

"I'd defend the reinstatement of the death penalty," he said. "Do you find that shocking?"

"I don't believe it."

"The death penalty makes a statement about our attitudes. It tells the ordinary citizen something about the society he lives in, that it's willing to confront evil and not evade it. It's a morality play, if you like, that tells us that life is a serious matter, that decisions are hard and costly, that perhaps we must perform a wrong act and hang a man in order to confront evil."

"It's barbaric."

"Yes, it is."

"An eye for an eye."

Jennifer moved away from him.

"Have you ever asked yourself what justice is?" he said.

"It's not a word I use much."

"But men have a hunger for justice. Most judges and lawyers avoid the issue and say they're just concerned with the working out of the law, but it's no accident that ordinary people talk about the courts and justice. When I was first appointed I spent some time thinking about what justice meant, what I was supposed to be doing. For the man on the street, it's as simple as the Mikado, "to make the punishment fit the crime," but what makes it fit? Justice is really an aesthetic concept, not a moral one at all. Fitness, fittingness. It must feel right. All this emphasis on therapy is corrupt. I have no business trying to cure people or even defining them as in need of cure. That's arrogant nonsense. Everything gets reduced to a repetitive and boring bit of medicine. Conditioning, all that foolishness. When I sit on the bench, I'm not my own man. I have an audience of all civilized men now and in the past, and I have to try to make decisions that reflect that."

"No-one," Jennifer said, "can honestly defend capital punishment unless he'd be prepared to be the hangman at his own son's execution."

"I've made you angry."

"Don't you ever feel uneasy," she said, "when you see a human being in front of you who's part of this ritual— because that's what you're talking about, a social ritual— and you suddenly realize that nothing in his attitudes or experience or capacity has any relationship with what he's going through? He's just some poor confused dope, blundering around. Because that's what criminals are really like."

"In the face of the law, they're no longer individuals. It isn't pragmatic."

"You talk about justice being aesthetic, but there's a hell of a lot of bad taste around. People, including judges, who see criminals as they've been taught by movies and television. Corrupt art. How can the ritual it nourishes not be

165

corrupt?"

She thought there was an edge to his voice as he answered.

"The decisions aren't simple or schematic, but if you throw away the vocabulary of two thousand years, refuse to talk about good or evil, just insist on talking about sickness and immaturity, you reduce us all."

They were sitting apart now, their bodies on separate sides of the bed, not touching. Jennifer felt naked and sat with her hands around her knees to cover herself.

"What does the audience of all civilized men think of you spending the weekend with me in this hotel?"

"That's a provocative question."

"Meant to be."

"Do you think I haven't asked it of myself?"

"Do the angels and sages turn their backs on weekends?"

"Why are you being so difficult?"

"I like to catch you in an inconsistency."

"I'm not on the bench now. I'm just a fallible human being."

"Is that a satisfactory answer?"

"No. I've discovered that I'm better at lying than I would have supposed, but I don't like it. It leaves a bad taste and I want it to stop."

His voice sounded cold, and Jennifer was frightened. The irritable desire to stick pins in him, to draw a little blood, was gone.

"I've just accepted a job in the Attorney General's department here in Toronto," he said. "I'm going to leave Eleanor. When things are settled, I hope you'll come and live with me."

His eyes were on her, but she turned away. She felt herself begin to shake. It was what she had felt last night, but worse. She closed her eyes to try and get control. She was dizzy and faint. She clasped her hands tight around her knees, but the shaking kept coming from somewhere inside; it wouldn't stop. Why was she breaking now? Her breath was coming more and more quickly, and she was afraid she was going to scream.

"What is it?" Tom was saying.

She shook her head, she couldn't speak. If he would keep talking, it might be better.

"Just take it easy, Jenny. Tell me what the trouble is."

His voice was helping. Her breathing began to slow a little. There were tears in her eyes now, but that was all right. She could let them come or wipe them away. She buried her face in her hands.

"I don't understand, Jenny. I thought you'd be pleased."

She was crying now, quietly.

"It's just all too much for me."

"You don't have to decide right away. There's lots of time for that."

She looked up and turned her face toward him. He reached out and wiped a tear off her face. He had wide flat fingers. She put her hand in his and tried to smile at him.

"Funny that I've survived all the bad news, but I felt as if the good news was going to finish me."

"Ever since the funeral, you've been looking exhausted."

"Maybe I am. I didn't realize."

"Your strength will come back."

"Tom, do you ever wonder if we can build a decent life out of broken promises."

"You have to build with whatever comes to hand."

"Barbara and I saw you at the concert last week."

"I know."

"Why didn't you mention it?"

"There was nothing to say. I can't discuss Eleanor with you. That may seem like a perverse and foolish bit of loyalty, but it's right to me."

"Does she know you're leaving?"

"I'm going to tell her tomorrow."

"How will she react?"

"I don't want to talk about it."

167

Jennifer knew it would be easier for her if the woman never became real, but she felt she must know something about her.

"I guess coming to Toronto would mean leaving my class at the hospital."

"There must be similar jobs here."

He was watching her face. She could feel tears starting again.

"I can't get used to the idea," she said, "of getting what I want. It seems wrong."

"Your protestant conscience."

"Are you leaving her because of me?"

"I'm leaving her because it's right. Being with you has given me some kind of hope for something better."

He put his arms around her. Something better. Could she believe in that? It was what she worked for with Melinda, with Jeffrey. To assert hope in the face of hopelessness. If she could maintain hope for Melinda, for Eugene, why not for herself?

"I've told them I'm taking the job. Tomorrow I'll tell Eleanor I'm leaving. That much is settled. I don't expect you to say this minute that you're going to come with me. I hope you will. I even think you will, but there are a lot of things for you to consider, your children, your job. We'll just tackle one thing at a time."

Jennifer couldn't speak, but she leaned forward and kissed him. Her strongest feeling was fear. She clung to him. They rolled over and made love, trying to lose all the complexity in the simple physical act, but consciousness never quite left her.

"I'm hungry," Tom said afterward. "Let's go and eat."

As they made their way to the restaurant, ordered and ate, Jennifer was lost. Everything was miles away. She was trying desperately, foolishly, to see into the future, to imagine what it would all be like. Leaving Kingston. Tom with the children.

Tom made conversation and she replied, then couldn't remember what either of them had said.

"Were you serious," she said, "in what you said about capital punishment?"

"Yes."

How could she live with a man with ideas like that? Or did it matter? How could she know what made a marriage good?

"Are you afraid of disagreements?"

"I guess so."

"In the most important way, we're not different," he said.

"What's the most important way?"

"We both care about it."

She sipped her wine. It was true, what he said, that they shared a concern for what could only be called their duty. Pompous word. Fat paunch of a word. They wanted to play the role of Citizen. Citizen Van Every and Citizen Mallen are shacked up in Toronto for a dirty weekend.

"Shall we go to a movie?" he said. "*Kamouraska*'s on nearby."

"I'd like to see that."

But when they got to the movie, she couldn't commit herself to it. It was a beautiful dark dream, but it didn't take her out of herself, only lay like a palimpsest of incomprehensible beauty over the struggle of her own feelings.

Coming out of the theatre, they held hands as they walked silently back to the hotel. In the cold darkness, Jennifer felt far from all the world except the man beside her, and everything was simple.

Back in the hotel, they undressed warily, climbed into bed and lay in silence, not touching. The future lay between them like a sword. Jennifer could hear the sound of traffic in the streets outside. She wanted to speak, but there was nothing to say. She could hear Tom's slow breathing. Was he asleep?

His hand touched her, moved down her arm. Her own hand met and clasped it, and they turned to face each other. He held her tight, pressing her against him until it hurt, then moved on top of her, and she spread her legs to receive him. Their bodies went their own way.

In the morning, they were gentle and careful, watched their words. They stayed on neutral ground. By afternoon, Jennifer was on the train to Kingston, and nothing had been said. She hadn't committed herself. Could she live with Tom? More to the point, perhaps, could she live without him? A few flakes of snow had begun to fall, and outside the window the lifeless fields passed by.

The house was empty when she got home. She wanted the children there. She changed her clothes, tidied a couple of rooms, tried to read. After eating a dinner of cold leftovers, she went to the basement and turned on the television set.

It was no wonder most of the programs were so bad. One so often watched when tired or preoccupied. She sat in front of the screen for an hour or so, expecting to hear the children arrive. The quiet sounds of the house made her more alone, but most of the time the television kept her from thinking. While she was watching a CBC play, she noticed a familiar face, thought at first it was an accident of features that this aging woman seemed known to her, then realized with a shock that it was Mary Todd.

They had known her in university. She had appeared in a lot of Hart House plays, and for a short while she went out with Robert's friend Peter Rowsome. It was one drunken evening during that period that Peter had confided to Jennifer that he was a homosexual, enjoining her to keep the secret even from Robert. She had never told anyone, not even Robert years later when they had met Peter and his wife Dorothy while they all lived in Toronto.

The grey pictures flickered in front of Jennifer's eyes. She no longer followed the story, only waited for Mary Todd's reappearance and stared at the face, trying to understand the mystery of this change. Her own face must look like that. Old. Before long the menopause. Why on earth did Tom want her?

The door upstairs opened, and she heard footsteps. She shouted hello and went to meet the children as they stood in the hall taking off their coats. She hugged the children, relieved, set at ease by the touch of their young bodies.

"Did you have a good time?"

"Great," Cindy said. "How about you?" Jennifer thought Cindy had guessed that she was meeting Tom, but she was not about to acknowledge it. "You two hungry?"

"We had supper late," Gavin said. "Hey. What skates and goes Ding Dong?"

"I don't know. What?"

"Avon Cournoyer."

"Where did you get that?"

"Dad told me."

Robert setting out to be the good father. It was touching to hear about his attempts.

"I was watching television. There's a play on with an old friend of your dad's and mine. Anybody want to watch it?"

"Is it half over?" Cindy said.

"At least that."

"I don't want to watch it then."

"I do," Gavin said. Jennifer thought he was saying it to please her. The two of them went down to the basement. She pointed out Mary Todd when she came on the screen.

"She's old."

"Do I look that old?"

"Of course not."

"She was in university when we were."

"She must have had a hard life."

It struck her now, watching, that Mary wasn't a very good actress. But what had Jennifer ever done that gave her the right to make harsh judgments? How few of that

171

group of students who felt the future giving way before their remarkable talents had done anything lasting? Mary had done better than most simply to go on practising her craft this long. The program came to an end, and Jennifer shipped Gavin off to bed and then went down to finish the ironing she had begun on Friday night. Tom was on his way back to the city, or talking to his wife.

The next day there was a shock for her at the hospital. Melinda had been taken to Toronto over the weekend. Only three children were brought in. There was no-one to turn to for a sense of accomplishment. Ten minutes into the class, Rennie wet her pants and began to cry in great blubbering sobs. Jennifer tried to take the opportunity to reinforce a couple of symbols, but Rennie was too upset. Jennifer tried to comfort her, then led her down the hall to find an orderly to take her for dry clothes and went back to mop up the floor. When she got back, George was bouncing Jeffrey's chair up and down, and Jeffrey was roaring with fear or anger. She made George sit back down and tried to get Jeffrey to use one of the symbols to express what he felt, but he refused, his eyes looking up from under the bony forehead in some kind of fierce silent rage.

Jennifer wondered if she could survive the class without Melinda. How long could she live in the dim suburb these children inhabited. She hated to think that McAdam might be right. Too easy, walking away from these children, saying nothing could be done, hiding in the arms of a man.

The orderly brought Rennie back, and the morning went on. In the afternoon, Jennifer was supposed to be setting up a test for some of the children in one of the wards to see if she could get results with the symbols that were different from the intelligence tests given by the psychologists. Instead perhaps she'd borrow Irving's car and drive to Napanee to visit Eugene. She wanted to do it soon while she still had the determination. She spent as long as she could working with Rennie. It was one of those days when

George was hopeless. It was all he could do to stay in a chair for a few minutes, and she let him play with the coloured charts in the corner of the room until he began to get wild and tear them. She worked on the simple concrete symbols with Rennie, trying to choose those that had some relationship to her experience. No point trying *house*, for Rennie hadn't lived in a house for years, not since her mother, herself retarded and found pregnant in a family who treated her as a domestic animal, had been run over by a truck passing their house on a country road. Hand, ear, eye; those were safe. Chair, wheelchair.

Jennifer and Irving were sitting over lunch when she asked him for his car.

"Sure you can have it. Slipping off for a little rendezvous in the country?"

"An elegant rendezvous in a jail with a former patient who seems to have adopted me."

"Slyfield."

"His mother phoned and bullied me into going to visit him."

"You didn't know him very well, did you?"

"I didn't think so, but he's decided I'm his friend. I don't seem to have any choice."

"Good of you to take him on. You must have better things to do."

"Other. I don't know about better."

She was close to telling Irving about Tom. It was terrible not having anyone to tell.

"What was the class like without Melinda?"

"Depressing."

"We'll have to cancel it soon."

"You mean McAdam will."

"Jenny, if you look at it carefully, you'll see he's right. We can't afford to keep that class running on some kind of absurd hope."

"What about Jeffrey? Given time I could reach him."

"If you want to spend the rest of your life on Jeffrey, adopt him."

Jennifer was taken aback by the remark. It was cruel and accurate. She could adopt him, if she was so determined to help, but she wouldn't. She sat silent as Irving's voice went on.

"You want magic, Jenny. All we can offer is hard work and a few opportunities, mostly small ones. A systematic professional approach. Lots of failures. Probably we'll never know what's going on inside Jeffrey, but he'll be fed and cleaned and kept warm as long as he lives. Maybe it would be better to have exposed him on a hillside at birth, but that's not the way we do things."

He gave her his car keys and told her where the car was parked. She collected her coat and went to it. She had thought of driving down Highway 2 to Napanee. It was a pleasanter drive but the jail was close to 401 so she went that way. She kept finding herself in borrowed cars.

Somewhere ahead of her, Eugene was locked in a cell, intoxicated by the belief that she could help him. Could she? And was Irving right that she expected magic? She knew that she couldn't cast out devils; it was not her gift.

The Regional Detention Centre was a low brick building with barbed wire around it. It was an unimpressive sight, but cleaner, no doubt, than some of the old county jails. Jennifer walked to the door and rang the bell. A tall grey-haired guard let her in and asked her business. She was left sitting on a bench in a bare corridor as he went off to summon Eugene for the visit. Everything here was clean and new. It was like the newer parts of the hospital. An empty functional place. Not the best environment for healing the soul.

What would Tom say about that? That it was simply punishment and the place didn't matter? But if, as he said, it was a play that was being played out, the setting ought to have some richness or grace or deep terror.

174

The guard gestured to her and led the way to a small room with three seats facing a counter and a glass wall. At each seat was a hole in the wall covered by wire. Do not touch lest you spread the infection of crime. Was it necessary? To prevent the passing of drugs and weapons. There must be some other, more humane way. Jennifer sat down on the farthest seat. Beside her a girl of perhaps sixteen, pregnant, was talking to a boy scarcely older who was dressed in the drab prison uniform. He was lean and muscular with a narrow unkind face. The girl wore a wedding ring.

Jennifer saw Eugene walking toward her window. He was smiling.

"I knew you'd come," he said as he sat down opposite her.

"How are you?"

"It's not that much worse than the hospital. Everybody here's crazy. Just have different symptoms."

Jennifer struggled to find something to discuss.

"Do you know your trial date?"

"April, so they say. Doesn't make much difference. They're going to find me guilty."

"Your state of mind may be some defence."

"I shoved it into her, that's all they want to know. That makes me the big bad wolf."

The bantering tone angered her. She remembered the girl in court.

"Think of how she must have felt."

"You women always stick together.

Jennifer had no answer. She wanted no part of this.

"When I get out, I'm going to get a place of my own. With a fence. I'll pay women to come there, and then I can do whatever I like."

"Where will you get the money?"

"My mother has money. She'll have to give it to me. So I won't rape any more innocent young girls. Don't you think that's a good idea?"

He was like a spider wrapping her round, trying to hold her paralyzed in the web of his sickness. She wouldn't join him.

"Those things sound like fantasies to me, Eugene."

"They sound like fantasies to you, do they Jennifer? Well that's good to know."

It was like the scene in her house three months ago, but here she should be able to leave; all she needed was to stand up and walk away, but his words had some power over her. She was alone with his madness.

"The whole thing is kind of pathetic when you think about it. It was my first time. I wanted to know what it was like. She should have just relaxed and let it happen. I tried to explain that I didn't want to hurt her. It wasn't anything to her."

Jennifer wondered whether to try and answer. Did it do any good to contradict him, try and bring him back to the real world?

"Can't you imagine what she might have felt, Eugene?"

"I'm not some kind of animal. I'm not insensitive."

"Then why did you do it?"

"I couldn't help it."

What she had said to Barbara. Eugene's eyes met hers, directly, simply.

"Do you think I'm dangerous?"

"Yes. Probably."

"I don't know what to do."

"Maybe the doctors can help."

"Do you believe that?"

"I don't know."

He brushed back his hair and exposed the scar on his head.

"What's that scar from?" she said.

"I shot myself."

"Were you trying to commit suicide?"

"Do you think I just wanted a scar to show off to the kids

at school?"

"When did it happen?"

"I was fourteen. I wish I'd known how to do it properly. Think of the trouble I'd have saved everyone."

"There's still a chance to make something of your life."

"Why do you say things you don't believe? I took you for an honest person."

The guard came to the young man who was talking to his pregnant wife and told them the visit was over. The girl started to cry and put her fingers through the wire to touch him before he was led away.

"What does your lawyer say about the trial?"

"He's going to try to get me sent to Penetang. Hospital for the Criminally Insane. That has a nice ring to it. You know, I've started compiling a list of important people who were nut cases. It's quite a long list."

"Do they let you have books in here?"

"Just the ones from their library. They're big on Zane Grey."

"Maybe the hospital could arrange to send your books on."

"You can try. It would be nice to have them."

A new couple had moved into the chairs on the left. The woman was heavy, country looking. The man was probably Jennifer's age, with a tattoo of a heart and an arrow through it on his forearm. They said a few words and then sat in silence. It made Jennifer more self-conscious.

"Do you ever get tired of being such a good person?" Eugene said. His voice was suddenly sharp and aggressive again.

"I'm not."

"Don't you ever feel a little crazy, as if you might go off the deep end?"

"I can't talk to you about that kind of thing. Eugene."

"Why not?"

"I guess I don't want to."

"You think I'm stupid. That I've never read anything."

"I know you've read a lot."

"But you don't really care. That's your kind of craziness. You pretend to care about people but you don't. You just like to fuck around in their minds. That's how you get your laughs. Why else would you come to see me?"

"Maybe you're right. If so, I can't do anything about it."

"Of course I'm right," Eugene said. He was almost shouting.

The guard appeared to tell Eugene the visit was over. Eugene ignored him until the man touched his arm and then pulled the arm violently away. The guard took hold of it tightly.

"You always have cops to take away people you're tired of. Where would you be without them? Just tell me that."

A second guard appeared. They were big men, and each one took Eugene by the arm and shoulder, and they marched him out.

The man and woman looked toward Jennifer as if she were to blame. He had fastened his guilt on her. He was a devil, and this bare institutional room was hell. Jennifer stood up from the chair. The man and woman followed her with their eyes as she went out. She was abandoning Eugene. As she abandoned Robert and Barbara and Jeffrey. But what else could she do? One of the uniformed guards opened a locked door for her, and she passed down the bare corridor. Alone.

She had the children. They would grow away from her. And Tom, perhaps Tom, but what would they become over the days and years? Nothing perfect or final. He was a mortal man, not a destiny. They would disagree and misunderstand. Nothing would ever conclude, only someday it would all stop. Why was she frightened? This random dance of atoms would not obey the laws of story-telling. What was it Robert like to quote? *Time is a child moving counters in a game. The royal power is a child's.*

The guard opened a second door, and she made her way out of the building. Outside, the air was full of huge white snowflakes that fell from the sky like a cold blessing.

Author's note: I owe a debt of thanks to Alan Gold for his guidance through the ways of the law and to Barbara Royds and Shirley McNaughton, who taught me a little about cerebral palsy and the Bliss symbols when I was doing research for a documentary film that never got made. Also to Dr. H. W. Cumming for medical information of other sorts. Needless to say, none of these people is responsible for the use I have chosen to make of the information they have given me. The characters in the book are wholly fictional and the hospital is not meant to be any real hospital, in Kingston or elsewhere.